★ ★ ★

SLAP YOUR SIDES

a novel by

M. E. Kerr

HarperTrophy®
An Imprint of HarperCollinsPublishers

Slap Your Sides
Copyright © 2001 by M. E. Kerr

Library of Congress Cataloging-in-Publication Data
Kerr, M. E.
    Slap your sides : a novel / by M. E. Kerr.
        p. cm.
    Summary: Life in their Pennsylvania hometown changes for Jubal Shoemaker
and his family when his older brother witnesses to his Quaker beliefs by becoming a conscientious objector during World War II.
    ISBN 0-06-029481-7 — ISBN 0-06-029482-5 (lib. bdg.)
    ISBN 0-06-447274-4 (pbk.)
    1. World War, 1939–1945—United States—Juvenile Fiction. [1. World War,
1939–1945—United States—Fiction. 2. Brothers—Fiction. 3. Conscientious
objectors—Fiction. 4. Quakers—Fiction.] I. Title.
PZ7.K6825 Sl 2001   00-054037
[Fic]—dc21   CIP
                                                               AC

Typography by Karin Paprocki

◆

First Harper Trophy edition, 2003

Visit us on the World Wide Web!
www.harperchildrens.com

★ ★ ★
PART ONE
★ ★ ★

★ ★ ★

If you want to win the war, clap your hands,
If your heart is with the corps,
    clap your hands,
If your heart is with the fleet,
    if you'll never face defeat,
Clap your hands! Clap your hands!
    Clap your hands!

This is Radio Dan, listeners, making an announcement I never dreamed would come over this or any other microphone in the U.S. of A.

You may already have heard that on April 9, 1942, just two days ago, 75,000 of our brave boys surrendered to the Japanese on Bataan.

It is the largest United States military force ever to surrender!

Listeners, in honor of those courageous servicemen, I am changing the name of this program to "Slap Your Sides."

We'll only clap our hands again when our soldiers, sailors, and marines are all safe and on their way back to us!

You will be hearing a new theme song, soon as we on the home front do all we can to help win this war.

And in that spirit, listeners, this broadcast will be sponsored by Wride Foods, which as you know has been transformed into a vital war industry.

Let's hear it for our guys: Slap your sides! Slap them hard! Slap your sides!

—Radio Dan broadcast, April 1942

★ ★ ★

ONE

I was thirteen the winter everything changed. I knew, even on the cold December night Bud left, that our family would never be the same again. Everyone was at the dinner table: Bud, me, Mom, Dad, my other brother, Tommy, and Hope Hart, from the next town over, Doylestown, Pennsylvania.

No one was saying anything except what began with "Please pass the . . ." I hated the way no one would talk about it, but not enough to mention it myself. Someone had left the radio on in the living room. We could hear Radio Dan signing off. He was a number-one cornball, but I listened to him sometimes, secretly. He was the only celebrity I had a personal acquaintance with, despite the fact that he wasn't always sure which Shoemaker kid I was. He lived down at the end of our street. He had this deep, friendly voice. You'd think he'd understand anything you told him. But I knew better. He wouldn't understand what Bud was doing, that was for sure.

My father got up, went in, and turned him off. He hardly ever listened to the radio anymore. Everything was about the war.

A rib roast, Bud's favorite, was being slowly eaten in

silence. Even Mahatma, our old collie, who favored Bud over all of us, seemed to sense something dire was taking place. He lay just outside the dining room, his eyes fixed on Bud.

When we finally left the house to take Bud to his train, Mom was crying and hanging on to him. Bud didn't want Mom to see him off. She said she'd send him some of her gingerbread and macaroons.

"I don't even know if we can get packages from home," Bud said.

"Of course you can!" Mom said.

Dad said, "Maybe he can't. We don't know how they feel about it."

"Well, he's not going to prison, Ef."

"No, he's not—and he's not going to Boy Scout camp, either."

"Ef, what a mean thing to say!"

"I didn't mean it mean."

"Don't send me anything, okay?" Bud said.

Mom cried out, "Come inside, Mahatma! You can't go with him!"

I thought I'd get to ride in back with Bud. I couldn't get used to Bud having a steady girl. He'd been with Hope almost two years, but I kept thinking it was like a case of measles or chicken pox—it'd go away in a while.

"Jubal, ride up here with me and Tom," Dad said to me.

Tommy put the radio on. There wasn't going to be any conversation on the way to the train.

In the back of the Buick, Bud and Hope were sitting so close, you'd think there were passengers on either side of them. They were holding hands. Earlier that evening Hope had given Bud a silver identification bracelet with their initials on the front and "MIND THE LIGHT" on the inside.

Hope Hart was a Goody Two-shoes and an optimist, the kind whose sunny ways wore you down eventually. She had hair a color in between red and brown, and brown eyes. She always knew the right way to walk in and out of rooms, and what to say in them. It was a skill Bud didn't have. He scowled his way through most social gatherings.

Hope was a year older than Bud, and she already had a college degree in home economics. I wanted to like her. I didn't want to blame her for everything that was happening to Bud.

"'Remember Pearl Harbor,'" a male chorus sang on the radio.

Dad snapped, "Shut that off!"

"I'll change the station," Tommy said.

"It'll be the same everywhere," Dad grumbled.

Tommy tried, got "Silent Night," tried again and got "White Christmas," tried again and got some news commentator saying production of automobiles had stopped and the factories were being changed over to airplane and tank factories. In a short time production of new radios for home use would be cut in half because the materials were needed for the war. Rubber, tin, and aluminum had become precious and were being saved for only the most important uses. Men's suits—

"Turn it *off*, Tom!"

"Yes, sir."

I glanced up at Tommy, and he gave me a weak smile. He was seventeen. Bud was twenty. I was the baby. But all of us looked alike. We all had thick black hair, sturdy builds, and the Shoemaker light-blue eyes.

Anyone in Sweet Creek could spot us as Efram Shoemaker's kids. E. F. SHOEMAKER was the sign over the only department store in town. My father called himself E. F. because he'd never liked the name Efram. Most people called him that, anyway. If you never liked the name, why did you give it to Bud, I'd asked him? Tradition, the answer came back. There'd been an Efram Shoemaker in Delaware County since the sixteen hundreds. Bud was Efram Elam Shoemaker. Elam after our grandfather, just as I was Jubal after our great-great-grandfather. Lucky for Tommy that our great-grandfather was named Thomas.

★ ★ ★

TWO

While my father parked the car, Tommy, Hope, Bud, and I went into the station.

When everyone sat down, I asked Bud, "Aren't you going to get a ticket?"

"I already have a ticket, Jube."

"When did you get it?"

"The government's paying his way," Tommy said.

"They are?" I was surprised. I thought that was the last thing the government would do: spring for a ticket for a conscientious objector.

"How long do you have to wait in New York before your train to Colorado?" Hope asked. She was wearing her hair pageboy style. She was in a red-plaid pleated skirt with boots and a white turtleneck sweater under a navy-blue pea jacket.

"It's just a few hours' wait," Bud said.

"But what will you do at this time of night?" Hope asked.

Bud tried a grin but didn't quite manage it. "There's always something to do in New York," he said, making it sound as though he knew all there was to know about Manhattan. He'd been there only once, years ago, for a Boy Scout jamboree.

Tommy said, "You could call Aunt Lizzie."

"I don't think she'd want me to call her," Bud said.

"Sure she would. You were always her favorite."

"Was," said Bud. "Now, who knows?"

Bud was the tallest, six foot four. He beat dad by two inches and Tommy by four. I was five five, still growing, but of all of us I was the muscle man . . . the strongest . . . the champion weight lifter at Sweet Creek Friends School. Although we three boys had gone to Quaker school, when Sweet Creek High was built, Tommy transferred because their basketball team was tops. Tommy was a top player.

Dad came in from the parking lot, and right behind him was Radio Dan and one of his kids.

If you didn't know Dan Daniel, you'd never expect that voice. He sounded like Orson Welles, Lowell Thomas, or any of the others who would keep you glued to the radio.

In person Radio Dan was plump and medium height, balding with a beer belly. He always wore polka-dot bow ties, blue ones, green ones, yellow ones. Were they clip-ons? He liked to wear V-neck sleeveless sweaters, the same color, with them. Under his right eye was a red birthmark shaped like Lake Ontario.

"Ssshoot!" Tommy said. "Radio Dan and Dean!"

"So act like who cares, " I said.

"Who does care?" Bud shrugged.

You had to cross a bridge to New Jersey to get to the Trenton train station. Everyone seemed to be saying good-bye at railroad or bus stations those days. There were uniforms everywhere. Some of the guys wearing them looked to me like kids dressed up to play war games in their backyards.

That's what Dean Daniel looked like that evening. This skinny boy dressed up like a Marine. His ears stuck out at the sides of his cap. He'd been my junior counselor in Cub Scout camp one summer, but he'd called for his folks to come and get him because he was terrified of spiders. Dean was a twin, but when you saw him with Danny Jr., they didn't even look like brothers. Danny Jr. looked tough, and he was.

The Daniels said hello to us and sat down on a bench nearby. Radio Dan was lighting a cigarette and passing the pack to Dean.

My father's ears were red. I'd always thought he wasn't comfortable with what Bud was doing. He'd never said as much, but I'd overheard conversations between Mom and him, and I'd heard him say he wasn't sure he'd have made the same decision.

"Is the train on time?" Dad asked Tommy. His voice was so low, Tommy had to ask him what he said.

He said it again, then shuffled his feet and stole a glance back at the Daniels.

Everyone in Sweet Creek knew about Bud, particularly Radio Dan. He knew all the town gossip. Nothing was secret for long in a town of twenty thousand. Bud had been asked not to lead his Scout troop last fall. When he drove up to Texaco in his old Ford, with the A gas rationing sticker on the windshield, the help took their time coming out to collect his coupon and gas him up. It was the same when he stopped at The Sweet Creek Diner for coffee, or went into Acme Food Stores for groceries. No one wanted to be of service to Bud Shoemaker.

"Please don't wait for the train," Bud said.

"We want to wait with you, Bud," Dad said.

"We're waiting," said Tommy.

"I don't want you to wait," Bud said.

I sang a little of "Wait Till the Sun Shines, Nellie," trying to provide some comic relief. But I knew there was no such thing as relief for Bud's situation. It was just going to get worse every day the war lasted.

I went into the men's, and Tommy followed me.

"I bet Dad hates having Radio Dan here!" Tommy said.

I knew that Tommy hated it too. Dean was home on leave from boot camp on Parris Island, South Carolina. Danny Jr., his twin, had joined the Marines when he was seventeen.

A few days ago Tommy and I had run into Dean in town. He was with his kid sister, Darie. She was my age but older-looking and -acting, the ways girls have of becoming people before boys do. She hadn't bothered to greet me, just stood there regarding me with these cool, bored eyes, as though in her short time on this planet she had rarely been subjected to an encounter with anyone as ordinary as I was.

Dean had punched his palm with his fist and told us

he couldn't wait to kill a Jap. Then he'd covered his mouth with his hand and said, "Whoops! Wrong person to tell that to!"

Tommy had shrugged and said, "I'm not partial to Japs."

"*You'd* never kill one, I bet!" Darie Daniel had piped up. She was always in Sweet Creek High plays, particularly the ones with music. Twice a night, there was a recording of her singing Radio Dan's theme song: "Slap Your Sides." I'd seen her in a few Gilbert and Sullivan operas. She was cocky and a little tomboyish, and she could belt a song so you'd hear it down to City Hall.

Tommy'd answered her, "I doubt I'd ever kill *anyone*."

"Even if someone was holding a gun to your mother's head?" Darie Daniel had said. "What would you do then?"

"I'd sic my bulldog, here, on him." Tommy had ruffled my hair and grinned down at me.

I remembered Bud had said the draft board had asked him those kinds of questions. What would you do if you saw a man raping a woman? Et cetera.

"Let's drop the subject," Dean'd said. "It's the last thing I want to talk about when I'm home on leave."

"I know how to shoot a gun," Darie Daniel had said. "And I'd have no compunction about blasting away if anyone dared hurt a member of my family!" She had a smart-aleck way about her, but she was cute; she could get away with it.

On the way back from town, Tommy had said, "This damn damn war!"

That night while he washed his hands beside me in the men's, Tommy muttered, "Radio Dan's going to mention this, wait and see!"

"Probably."

"At least Darie wasn't with them."

"Who cares about Darie?"

"I have to go to school with her," said Tommy. "You don't."

"It's Bud I feel sorry for," I said.

"Nothing fazes Bud as long as he's got Hopeful." Tommy laughed.

"That's the truth," I said.

When we came back out, Tommy checked on Bud's train and called out, "Track Three. All aboard, Bud!"

The Daniels got up too. There was only one train heading for New York.

I was watching a woman in a fur coat hanging on the arm of a soldier. I remembered when Aunt Lizzie had sent Mom a coat one winter, saying she'd bought it on sale and couldn't return it. She didn't fool Winifred Shoemaker. My mother knew that was Lizzie's way of sharing her good fortune with her sister. Aunt Lizzie's husband was a successful artist, and she had a good job in advertising. My mother had no sooner taken the coat from its box and shaken out the wrinkles than Bud had snapped open his Scout knife and cut off the fur collar.

"Mom, you don't want animals killed so your neck can be warm, do you?" He'd tossed the fur in the wastebasket.

"I'd like to be asked first, Bud," Mom had said.

"Next time I will. I promise."

But he wouldn't. Dad claimed Bud had a self-righteous streak. Once some hunters had left dead fowl in their station wagon and gone back to the woods to shoot more. Bud had passed the car, and he'd taken the pheasants, brought them home, and buried them in the backyard.

"How do you know they weren't planning to have pheasant for their suppers?" Dad had asked. My father was not against hunting for food on your table.

"They were going to sell them!" Bud had insisted.

"How do you know, Bud?"

"I just know."

Suddenly, servicemen seemed to come from everywhere, all heading for Track 3.

Dad stopped and held up his hand. "We'll say our good-byes here."

He hugged Bud and then Tommy did.

"I'll write you, Bud," I said. I was in tears.

Bud bent down and held me tight. "You take care of Mom," he said. "And Hope. "

"Okay, I will."

"You and Tommy help the Harts with those horses, okay? And take special care of Quinn."

"I will," I promised. Quinn was a chestnut gelding, Bud's favorite of all the horses the Harts boarded or held for sale.

"I'll write you from Colorado," Bud said.

Radio Dan and his boy had stopped a few feet away.

"Take care of yourself, son!" that fabulous voice rang out.

I could hear Hope whispering to Bud, "I love thee. I'll wait for thee, Bud, for as long as need be."

"And I love thee."

They were speaking the old-fashioned "plain language" some Friends still used with family and at meetings.

Nobody in our family had used it until Bud met Hope when he took the summer job on their farm. After that I would hear Bud speak it nights on the telephone. *I think of thee all the time.*

As a young man Dad had not thought of himself as a strict Quaker. He wasn't a regular at the meetinghouse. His family way back was; then he was when he met my mother. Tommy was a lot like Dad. But Bud and I were believers. We would never have considered a school that wasn't Quaker. Bud chose to go to Swarthmore College. Sometimes when he was home and would speak at Sweet Creek meeting, I would hear how serious he was about religion. I would be surprised at Bud's anger, telling off Friends at meeting, saying they were some of the most successful businessmen in the county, but did they tithe, did they give ten percent of their earnings to Friends? Bud bet not! His eyes were fire, and I would be amazed. I also worried that I wasn't as strong as Bud. When it came my time to register for the draft, what kind of a Quaker would *I* be?

My dad said that it was a good thing Bud had found Hope. Hope, he had said, was more like Bud than Bud was. The whole Hart family were passionate Quakers, a bit on the humorless side.

After our good-byes we left Hope standing alone with Bud, locked in this long kiss.

Radio Dan headed for the exit too, then paused to light another cigarette.

"What's going to happen to Bud *now*?" I asked my father, keeping my voice down. "Will he have a job?" I knew that because Bud was a conscientious objector, he was going to a Civilian Public Service camp. But I was still in the dark about what would become of him next. I had the feeling he didn't know himself.

"Wait until we get home."

E. F. Shoemaker Company and radio station WBEA were on the same side of Pilgrim Lane, a few doors from each other. Tuesdays Dad and Radio Dan went to Rotary together. Before Rotary, Dad would stop by the radio station to pick up Radio Dan and walk down to Sweet Creek Inn with him, for the luncheon meeting.

And there the two of them were in Trenton: one seeing his second son off to war, and Dad seeing Bud off to Colorado, about as far away from any war as he could get.

When Hope caught up with us, for the first time her eyes had a watery look, but she was holding her chin up, smiling.

She said, "Bud's going to be fine!" Then, probably for Radio Dan's benefit, "I'm so proud of him!"

Tommy held the door open for her. "He's lucky he's got you."

Behind me Dad made a strange sound somewhere between a hum and a low groan.

★ ★ ★

THREE

Aunt Lizzie didn't have any qualms about wearing furs. She handed my father what had once been a fox, with black button eyes and a bushy fur tail.

"How's Bud doing?" she asked my father.

"Fine! He's getting lots of exercise, cutting down trees, clearing forests."

"In freezing weather," my mother added.

"Worse than this weather?" Lizzie laughed. She was always teasing Mom about the weather in Pennsylvania, complaining that it was a sacrifice to drive all the way from New York City to Sweet Creek every Christmas.

"If you don't like the weather, come another time. The twenty-fifth of December isn't special to me," Mom said. She said it every year; she enjoyed telling everyone how Lizzie and she grew up with no fuss at Christmas. The only important day on Quaker calendars was First Day, Sunday.

"Nothing's worse than this weather!" my cousin Natalia grumbled. "Damnation!"

Aunt Lizzie said, "What did I tell you about saying 'damnation'?"

"Not to."

"Then don't."

"The weather's plenty worse where Bud is," said Mom. "Bud's in Colorado."

"I know where he is. You gave me his address, remember? I sent him a couple pounds of fudge from Schrafft's."

"He'll love that, Lizzie," Mom said.

"Poor Bud," said Lizzie.

Tommy was bringing in their luggage, snow dusting his black curls and his coat collar. Natalia couldn't take her eyes off him. I felt like telling her she had a snowball's chance in hell of getting to first base with Fast Tom. That was Bud's nickname for him. I had to be polite and pretend Fast Tom would even *look* at someone fourteen, who was five foot two and about one hundred and fifty pounds.

My father said to Lizzie, "Around here we're not thinking of Bud as 'poor Bud.'"

"Well I'm not from around here, Efram."

"When in Rome . . ."

But it wouldn't do any good to remind Lizzie she was in Efram Shoemaker's home and should abide by his rules.

Lizzie always told Bud, Tommy, and me not to call her "Aunt," to call her Lizzie. Her husband, Mike Granger, was Jewish and didn't care to celebrate the holidays, so he stayed behind with their four Siamese cats. They lived in Greenwich Village, once described by my father as "full of bohemians who believe in free love." I'd asked Tommy what free love was, and Tommy had said it was going to bed with someone you weren't married to. Mike and Lizzie rented apartments in their town house to writers and musicians, and for years I pictured a place filled with paintings and pianos, mattresses strewn about on the floors, and you-know-what going on day and night.

I thought of Lizzie as insanely glamorous. I didn't care that she wore a dead animal around her neck. She was blond like Mom, but thinner and more stylish. She had these peekaboo bangs that made her look like the actress Veronica Lake. Tommy and I had seen Veronica Lake in *This Gun for Hire*. Tommy had leaned over and whispered to me, "She can put her shoes under my bed any day."

Mike Granger was an artist with long black hair and a bushy black beard. As kids, Mom and Lizzie had always been close in age, sentiments, and proximity. Then Lizzie went to Lake Placid, New York, one summer to work as a waitress and earn money for college. She picked a resort where Mike taught art to the guests. After that the sisters' lives were as different as fishes' and birds', with Lizzie doing the flying.

Also different as fish and birds were Lizzie and her daughter. I used to believe that if I closed my eyes and just heard Natalia without seeing her, I would think she was older than fourteen and not fat. She was a big talker. Sometimes there was a certain edge of sophistication to things she said. Then it would be spoiled when I watched her pop four marshmallows into her mouth at one time. She would talk with her mouth full, too, as though she realized eating was going to be of prime importance in her life, so she'd better learn early how to eat while she did other things.

I had promised my mother that when Natalia went up to bed, I would go too, so she didn't feel she was missing anything downstairs.

She would sleep on a cot in the sewing room, and Lizzie would sleep on the studio couch.

Bud, Tommy, and I shared a room. I knew that soon Natalia would wander down to visit. I hadn't bothered to shut the door. I hadn't changed into pajamas, either.

She was wearing this long silk nightie, with Bud's terry-cloth robe over it. It had been too heavy for him to pack. Natalia had not only a manicure with bright-red nails, but also a pedicure in the same color. She had something in a paper bag.

"Do you like bonbons?" She held the bag out to me.

"I can't eat any more."

"Only *one* pie," she said, referring to the pumpkin pie Mom had made for dessert. "You should see what *we* have for dessert when we're home. Several different kinds of pies or cake, and then something exotic like flan."

I was not going to ask her what flan was. I said, "How come you have so many cats?"

"They're not just cats. They're Siamese. They're very chic."

"Why?"

"They just are. Everybody knows it. . . . Mummy wanted to give them Oriental names, but I said that was the most obvious thing I'd ever heard, and Daddy said over his dead body!"

"So what did she name them?"

"She didn't. Daddy did. He named them Marx, Freud, Einstein, and Shakespeare. Do you know why?"

"How would I know why?"

"Because Daddy says they gave us the best things in life."

Natalia bent over to get a glimpse of Mahatma, who was under Bud's bed. She said, "Mahatma, you were named after a man of conviction too!"

Stapled to Bud's desk blotter was a typewritten quote from Mahatma Gandhi: *Nonviolence and truth are inseparable. . . . There is no God higher than truth.* Years ago Bud had won the senior essay contest at SCFS writing about Gandhi.

Over Tommy's desk was the sheet music to "I Surrender, Dear," showing a silhouette of a female naked from the waist up. Thumbtacked to that was a photograph of Lillie Light, who hadn't surrendered to Tommy yet. I knew because Tommy kept a secret graph of how far he got with a girl. He hadn't hit the 100 mark with one yet, and he was only to 30 with Lillie.

Natalia exclaimed, "That dog has become pathetic! He doesn't even wag his tail!"

"He misses Bud. That makes two brokenhearted

beasts. Mahatma and Quinn, this horse at a farm where we help out."

I'd watched Bud groom Quinn as a way of saying good-bye the day before he left. He not only brushed and curried him, but he clipped his fetlocks and the edges of his ears. Then he scrubbed him and shampooed him, and when he was done, I saw Quinn lift his head, eye Bud, snort, and dance a little.

Ever since, Quinn had been nickering for Bud, same as he'd nickered for his owner who'd boarded him there through the war.

Natalia said, "Did you hear the one about the absentminded professor?"

"No."

"The absentminded professor unbuttoned his vest, took out his necktie, and wet his pants."

I said, "Ha, ha, ha," hating it that my face had turned red.

Natalia reached into the bag and put a bonbon into her mouth. "Mum said not to tell you any jokes, that you'd be shocked."

"Oh, sure. Lookit me. I'm shocked." I widened my eyes and made my mouth an O.

She said, "Do you know how porcupines make love?"

"No."

"V-er-y carefully!"

"V-er-y funny," I said.

"Who sleeps in the top bunk?" Bonbons #3, #4, and #5.

"I do. Bud sleeps on the single bed."

"Which brother do you like most?"

"I like both the same. But I'm more like Bud." I actually prayed that I *could* be more like my older brother. Before the war I didn't think about it very much, but after we were attacked at Pearl Harbor, it was always on my mind. Was it fair that other guys would have to fight those Japs and the Shoemaker men wouldn't?

Natalia was in the doorway, her hand in the bag of bonbons, her mouth full of them. "Does Bud say thee like Quakers?"

"Sometimes he does, but we don't."

"It's the farthest thing from my mind that you *would*. Mum says Bud's a *dedicated* Quaker, which is why he's a conchie."

I'd heard Bud called a slacker, but I'd never heard the expression "conchie" before.

"He's dedicated about the big issues, " I said, "but he likes a beer now and then. And he doesn't have my mother's strict views of Christmas or things like that."

"What about Tommy?"

"Tommy's Tommy."

"Yes," Natalia purred. "He is. . . . Well, thee have a good night."

"Thee have one, too," I told her.

"Don't you *love* saying thee, Jubal?"

I shrugged, because I didn't even like it.

I hadn't had anything against the "plain language" until Bud started speaking it with Hope. I couldn't help thinking that she made it easy for Bud to choose the conscientious objector classification, 4E. She wouldn't have it any other way. Yet a lot of Quakers just became 1AO, which meant they would go into the service but not into combat. It would have been easier for everyone if Bud had chosen that route, but with some thanks to Hope, Bud wasn't about doing what was easy.

"Thee have a good sleep," said Natalia, finally leaving.

"Okay. Thee too."

I waited until I heard her door close. Then I shut mine and said my prayers.

On Sunday morning Hope was planning to come from Doylestown to the Sweet Creek meeting. Even though no one was supposed to decide beforehand what they got up to talk about, Hope had already planned to have her say about something. Mom said she hoped Bud and Hope were not going to marry; it wasn't good to begin a marriage living apart.

I hoped they wouldn't marry for a different reason. I felt like I was losing Bud, and she was part of the reason.

When I couldn't sleep, I turned on the radio. Radio Dan was saying someplace called Wake Island had been heavily bombed by a group of our Flying Fortresses. Some 75,000 pounds of bombs had been dropped. "But the good Lord be thanked, there were no casualties."

I wondered if Bud let himself know what was going on in the war.

I could almost hear Bud say, How can you drop that many bombs without casualties? There're casualties, if you count the people you're bombing!

But I felt good about the news. Maybe the war would be over next year.

When Tommy came barging into the room, I was almost asleep. After he got into his pajamas, he prayed on his knees, whispering in that way he had so you almost heard the words, but you never really did.

I didn't want to get really awake, so I let him think I was sound asleep.

When he was finished praying, he fiddled with the radio dial for a minute. In between all the songs about waiting for somebody, missing somebody, and spending nights alone were the ones about the war itself. Stuff like "Good-bye, Mama (I'm Off to Yokohama)" and "Praise the Lord and Pass the Ammunition!!" He finally turned it off.

Then I heard him say, "Oh, all right!" and the dog tags around Mahatma's neck rattled as he climbed into bed with Tommy.

★ ★ ★

FOUR

"Lizzie, would you mind coming to the Sweet Creek
meeting with our family this morning?"

Lizzie shot my mother a look. She and Natalia
were both dressed and ready to be dropped off at Second
Presbyterian church, as usual.

"Your service is so plain, Win. If I go to a church,
I like to sing. I love the Christmas decorations—the
candles and the pine branches."

"Just this once," my mother persisted.

"I respect your beliefs, Winnie. While I'd love a
Christmas tree on Christmas, I understand. I haven't
lost my memory of Mama saying *every* day is special
and we don't need to make one day more important than
the next, unless it's First Day. I can hear her telling us
that, when we were little girls. But Win, tell me why
Natalia and I have to go somewhere and sit in silence,
when that's not our faith? Our family isn't religious."

My father said, "Let them go where they want to!"

"I wouldn't mind going to the Quaker church,"
Natalia said.

"It's not a church," her mother said. "It's a big room
with hard benches, no backs to them. You sit there and
say nothing. I don't think you could stand it, Natalia!"

"We'll drop you off at the Presbyterian church," my father said. "Come along."

But then Mom said, "This year I'd be pleased if all the family came together for Bud."

"I'll do it," Natalia said. "Mom?"

The meetinghouse was packed. Even the facing benches were full by the time the silence began. You were supposed to "center down" and get in touch with what was inside you. You were supposed to connect with your own light. "MIND THE LIGHT," which Hope had had engraved on Bud's ID bracelet, just meant to follow your heart.

From across the street came the faint sounds of the Catholic choir singing in Latin. I closed my eyes and tried not to hear their music. We had none. Radio Dan was Catholic. I thought of him and Mrs. Daniel over there with Darie, the only kid they had left to kneel down with them. In their front window was the service banner with two blue stars on it. Those banners were everywhere in Sweet Creek. There were even a few gold ones, which meant that old man Chayka had probably been the one to deliver the Western Union telegram announcing someone's death in the war. There weren't any messenger "boys" in Sweet Creek anymore. Anyone old enough to work who'd been turned down by the armed forces could have his pick of jobs.

That was why Tommy and I had joined Bud working for Hope's father all summer, helping him and Luke

Casper tame and exercise the horses. The Harts had always been dairy farmers. When Luke Casper, their neighbor, had to fold his farm, he talked Mr. Hart into buying and boarding horses. Luke would teach him the business.

Bud used to worry because Luke sometimes drank and got careless, and Hope's brother, Abel, was just naturally careless. Abel didn't have the patience to load the trailer correctly. He'd forget the horses' shipping boots, or their head bumpers. Luke Casper would complain to Bud that Abel would blanket the horses wet after rides, that all he wanted to do was read his books up in the hayloft.

The morning's silence seemed heavy to me, probably because I dreaded the idea Hope could be announcing a coming marriage to Bud. Usually couples appeared together to say their intentions, but if one was away, as Bud was, it could be done by the other.

Hope had brought Abel with her. She sat with Mom and Natalia in the women's section, opposite us males. Friends who weren't looking Hope over were staring at Abel. He had fire-red hair, brown—almost black—eyes, and pale white skin. He wasn't what you'd call fat, but he was tall and chunky, with the kind of build a football halfback might have. Abel almost never smiled. He was always biting his lips, or blinking, as though he didn't have all his marbles. He had a reputation for being a crusader, protesting when factories hired scabs, picketing

The Palace and The Strand in Sweet Creek because they made Negroes sit upstairs.

I was eager for Hope to make her move. There was no minister, of course. We didn't recognize one person having authority over another. We didn't have stained-glass windows or candlelight or incense. Friends got up when the spirit moved them. I'd been in meetings when no one spoke. To me they were the most boring. I'd also been in meetings when someone went on and on and made no sense. You had to sit there and listen. If you closed your eyes, you could be accused of sleeping.

Soon Hope was on her feet. She was pushing back a strand of her long auburn hair, which never stayed back. She was waiting until she had everyone's attention.

"Friends," she began, "you may have seen me at your meeting before. I'm a member of the Doylestown meeting, but I came here several times with Efram Shoemaker, known to all of you as Bud.

"As many of you know, he's now in a Civilian Public Service camp in Colorado. Some people say well, why didn't he just register as a 1AO and serve as a noncombatant? . . . *Some* people ask that. Most Quakers know the answer. If you load the bullet in the gun, or shoot the gun, or carry away the one shot by a gun, you are at war. If you join the military and do little more than paperwork in some office down in Richmond, Virginia, you are at war. . . . Bud chose to be a witness against this war, against war of any kind, for any reason!"

I could see many Friends nodding their heads in

agreement with Hope.

"As a 4E conscientious objector he will perform work of national importance, unconnected with the war, serving without pay, in whatever capacity he is assigned, for however long is necessary."

Hope pushed that same strand of hair back.

Across from her, Abel had this dizzy little smile on his face. He often looked as though he heard voices or was under some kind of spell. Even when a new horse arrived on the Hart farm, it was wary of him, would pull away or squeal when he tried to handle it. Horses always know if you're strange.

"I am asking for your prayers," Hope continued, "to keep Bud strong and confident. But I am also here to thank you. I believe a lot of the credit for Bud's peace testimony can go to you and this meetinghouse.

"Thank you. God bless you."

Natalia clapped, and heads turned to see who was rude enough to applaud.

Lizzie bent down and said something to her about it.

Slim Hislop waited another fifteen minutes to get up. He had been the caretaker of the meetinghouse for years, until his knees went on him. He said he'd known Bud since he was a little kid and even then Bud had been special. He elaborated: Bud gave his toys to the flood relief one spring, "and I mean his toys, all of them," on and on through Bud becoming an Eagle Scout, up to the day Bud filled out Form 47. He returned it to the draft board, writing that the dictates of his personal conscience forbade him to participate in war, in any form, because he believed man was destined to increase and improve, not to decrease and destroy.

I felt tears behind my eyes. I wished Bud was there to hear someone finally saying something good about him. I was glad for the Sweet Creek meeting, for the Friends there, for the company of other people who appreciated what Bud stood for.

Suddenly Aunt Lizzie was on her feet. The fur cape had dropped to the highly polished plain wooden floor. Lizzie stood there in her dark-green Peck & Peck suit with the white silk blouse and the sprig of holly in her lapel. Her blond hair was pulled back in a chignon. I knew probably no one approved of her makeup or her brightly colored clothes, but I believed as Dad did: It didn't hurt. Who did it hurt? I think I even liked it. The Sweet Creek meetinghouse could use a little glamour. I *was* surprised that Lizzie was going to say something; amazed, really. Yet I'd always suspected Bud was her favorite.

"Friends, I know you welcome anyone who wants to speak, and I feel obliged to.

"As a young girl I came to this meeting, and this morning when my sister, Winifred Shoemaker, asked me to join the family here, I did *not* want to do it. I'll tell you that right up front. I could have gone to the Presbyterian Church and been happy singing the old Christian hymns without my conscience waking up. I could have said my prayers to keep my nephew, Bud Shoemaker, safe and well, and that would have been that."

I couldn't help smiling a litttle. She had everybody's attention, even Abel's. Lizzie always made an impression.

"Friends, I once considered myself a Quaker. This was my home meeting, as some of you know. But then I fell in love and 'married out.' I am married to a man who is Jewish. Over the twenty years of our marriage I have come to know his relatives and many of his friends. We are lucky to be living in America, and if we were *not*, my husband, and his relatives and friends, would be in concentration camps at best. More likely they'd be dead.

"As Christian people aren't you concerned about the mass murder in Europe? Don't you listen to the news? Don't you know what's going on over there? Haven't you heard of Adolf Hitler? How can you expect other people to risk their lives in a war that affects every single one of us?

"Friends, I have to speak up and oppose this praise for a conchie, even though he is my own blood. I may love Bud Shoemaker, but I don't admire him any longer. How can I if he won't pull his weight in this war? How can you be pacifists with a madman like Hitler ready to rule the world? I want to say to you all, Wake up!

"Thank you."

FIVE

We headed away from the meetinghouse in silence. There was a strong odor of onions in the air, coming from Wride Foods. Before the war they made mayonnaise and potato salad, but the government stepped in and changed their entire operation. Now they dehydrated onions for K rations.

They were Radio Dan's sponsor.

Tommy had listened to the program for a few days, to see if Bud would be mentioned during one of Radio Dan's meandering musings. Dan would say whatever popped into his head, but according to Tommy the power of Rotary prevailed. Radio Dan wasn't going to go after the son of a fellow Rotarian.

My father always made a stop at his store on the way back from meeting. He would get out and check that the doors were locked. Because he had locked them himself on Saturday night, he never found them unlocked. That did not stop him.

"Please hurry, Efram," Lizzie said. "I have to go to the little girls' room."

"You can use the facilities at the store." Those were the first words he'd spoken to Lizzie since we'd all come out of meeting.

"Never mind, I'll wait."

"Suit yourself, Lizzie," he said from the driver's seat, and then in an aside he said quietly, "You always do."

"No, I do not always suit myself, Efram Shoemaker! I come here every single year to spend the holidays with my sister, since she won't leave *you* alone at Christmas, and *you* can't leave that department store of yours!"

"So that was what *that* was all about, back at the meetinghouse!" asked my father. "Getting even?"

"Maybe if you ever listened to the news, you'd know what it was all about!"

"I read the newspapers. That's enough."

My mother edged into the conversation. "It's just too bad that what you had to say came on top of what Hope had to say."

"What Hope said was half the reason I had to get up!" Lizzie said.

"This isn't a war about the Jews!" my father said. "It's a war about German expansionism!"

"Those are just words, Efram! The Jews are being killed!"

"They're not the only ones."

Mom said, "Can we *please* not talk about the war?"

"I'm so hungry I could eat a bear!" Natalia complained.

My mother made the suggestion to my father that we drive straight home.

"We're two seconds away," he said.

"You *know* the doors are locked, Ef."

"It might be this very morning they're not, Winnie."

He was already pulling into a parking space in front of the store.

I was the first to speak. "Someone soaped the windows."

My father had the Buick's door open, but he just sat there looking at what was written in soap.

"Oh, Efram," said my mother softly.

"What does it say?" Natalia asked.

Everyone was still a moment while they read:

YOUR SON IS A SLACKER

SIX

The window soaping had punched the breath out of Dad. He'd said it was "disheartening," and all that Sunday I could see his eyes close to tears. He knew people in Sweet Creek disapproved of Bud's choosing to be a CO, but I don't think he ever expected anyone to slander Bud right there on our store windows, some unknown someone, like a thief in the night.

Next day, just as Lizzie and Natalia were leaving, my father cleared his throat the way someone has of doing it even though nothing's there. He was working himself up to saying, "Lizzie, I don't intend to write Bud about your little speech at the meeting, and I hope that *you* won't write Bud about the soaping of my store windows. I don't like to worry him."

"I already wrote him about both things," Tommy piped up. "Bud wants to know what's going on here. He doesn't want to be spared."

"You wrote him already?"

"I write him every day. . . . I mailed it this morning."

"Then that's that," said my father.

"I would *never* have written Bud about your windows," Lizzie said. "Did I say anything about it when we talked with him on the phone?"

"You didn't have a chance," Natalia said. She had a pair of Tommy's socks in her suitcase. I'd let her take them. That would have made Bud smile, anyone wanting Tommy's stuff for a souvenir, but I didn't dare write him about it. I wasn't sure Bud wouldn't tell Tommy. There was something mysterious going on suddenly between Tommy and Bud.

When Bud called that afternoon, we all took turns. He called three days *after* Christmas because most servicemen were calling home for the holidays, or trying to. He felt obliged to give them priority. He was keeping his call short for the same reason.

He said what he'd been saying in letters: that he liked the other guys, that it was beautiful where he was, that he was becoming an expert at wood chopping. Then he thanked Lizzie for the Schrafft's candy, and when it came my turn, he made slurping noises and said, "Here's a big sloppy kiss, little bro." Bud and Tommy used to gang up on me and give me these icky dog kisses with their tongues.

The family had already received two letters from Bud, but there had also been a third, addressed to Tommy. On the front and back of the envelope PERSONAL was printed out in block letters and underlined.

No one had asked Tommy about it.

My folks must have felt it wasn't their business: It was something between brothers. But *I* felt left out. I was afraid if I opened my big mouth, Tommy would tell me to buzz off.

"Honey, I hope the cat's better when you get home," said my mother, hugging Aunt Lizzie.

"Thanks, sis."

Uncle Mike had called the night before to say he'd come home to find one of Freud's eyes closed and bloody.

Natalia said, "I wish I had all the money Freud has cost us at the vet. I'd be rich."

"It's Shakespeare's fault. He pounces on poor Freud the moment Freud falls fast asleep," said Lizzie.

We stood around in the doorway saying good-bye. They had stayed just three nights. Dad had come home early from the store for Bud's call, and to bid them farewell.

I had plans for when they left. I was going to find that letter Bud had sent to Tommy. Mom and Dad would take Mahatma for a walk before it got dark. He was heart-broken, hanging out under Bud's bed or sitting by the door, expecting him to come through it any minute.

Tommy was catching the bus to visit Lillie Light, probably hoping he could reach 40 on her graph. Before he left, he held his arms out and spun around, showing off his new topcoat and hat. They were Lizzie's Christmas presents from Natalia and her. She said maybe certain Quakers didn't believe in featuring December twenty-fifth over any other day, but she wasn't a Quaker anymore. She came laden down with gifts.

She knew that Tommy and I always wore Bud's hand-me-downs. Her gifts to me were both war sto-ries: Hemingway's *For Whom the Bell Tolls* and *The*

Moon Is Down by John Steinbeck. I loved to read, the same way Tommy loved to draw. I didn't care much about clothes.

Tommy did. He took after Dad that way. Dad claimed that he represented E. F. Shoemaker Company and was obliged to look his best. But Dad spent more money on clothes than Mom did, and he worked out at the YMCA three nights a week. Watching him put the finishing touches on what he was wearing, in front of a mirror, never left any doubt that Dad was a little stuck on himself.

I think Tommy knew, too, that he was getting this great face. As much as we all looked alike, put some cheekbones here, and move the eyes there, and the differences were startling when it came to Tommy.

I knew it when I thought about it, and when my cousin wanted his socks for souvenirs, but living every day with him, I didn't pay that much attention.

"What do you think of me?" he said.

He had on this herringbone tweed coat, and a soft brown fedora with a small red feather in the hatband.

"You look sharp."

"Do I?" He was smiling and still twirling around, his eye catching himself in the mirror across the parlor.

"You got handsome," I said.

"No, I didn't!" He blushed. "It's just the clothes Lizzie got me."

He left the house with this big grin, and I waited until he was out of sight.

On Tommy's desk was one of the new paperback books Judge Edward Whipple had donated to every boy in the junior and senior classes at Sweet Creek High. *The Red Badge of Courage* by Stephen Crane.

I'd read it last summer. I'd never forget the first sentence. It sent chills down my spine.

> *The cold passed reluctantly from the earth, and the retiring fogs revealed an army stretched out on the hills, resting.*

But at Friends School we'd laughed about the fact that Crane had never been to war. Only somebody who'd never been shot at would think of a wound as a "red badge of courage." Besides, he'd bragged that he'd written the book in just "ten nights."

My family knew the Whipples very well. My father said one of the reasons the draft board hadn't given Bud that hard a time about his choice to be classified 4E was because the judge knew him and never doubted his sincerity.

Shortly after Judge Whipple presented all those books to SCHS, a Lancaster Mennonite named Gish, along with Lillie Light's father, arranged a showing of the movie *All Quiet on the Western Front*. School kids were bussed to see it. Lew Ayres, the movie star who played the lead, became a CO years after he made that picture. That was right after Pearl Harbor, before Sweet Creekers were really involved in the war. It was before Radio Dan had begun calling himself The Home Front

Man. Up until then he'd just been a disc jockey, and he'd called his program "Clap Your Hands."

I found the letter I was looking for in Tommy's lower desk drawer.

Dear Tommy,

We went out to do some caroling before Christmas. There were six of us, five Catholics and Quaker Bud. Thanks to you, I knew the words to almost all the carols. Remember how you'd play them at Christmas and Mom would forget she didn't feature Christmas and hum them?

We'd decided to serenade the houses up on the ridge, about eight of them, mostly poor families with kids, we'd been told. We did it for the kids, really.

It was bitter cold and snowing a little. Porch lights went on, and we could see people looking out the windows. We were carrying small candles in paper cups.

At one house they blinked the lights when we were done as though they were saying thanks. And at another, a woman opened the door a crack and called out, "Merry Christmas!"

At the third house a man came out on the porch in boots and a leather jacket, and he shouted while we were singing, "Where you boys from?" We just kept on singing, so he came down the porch steps, and we saw he was carrying a pistol.

"I *said* where you boys from?"

My buddy, Cal, said we'd better get out of there fast, so we called "Merry Christmas!" over our shoulders. But he was hollering that he knew where we were from and he'd like to kill us! Then he began firing the pistol.

We beat it, and thank God he didn't chase after us, but by the time we got down to the next house, there were a man and woman in the doorway telling us, "Go away! We don't want your kind on our property!" Same kind of thing at the next house, so guess who probably telephoned them we were coming. More vile names for us as we kept going, and one guy came out carrying a baseball bat, promising to bust open our skulls.

Tommy, I'm not telling you this for sympathy. It was our own fault for not knowing better. In the hills here, outside Saw Hill, we almost forgot how people feel, but we are learning.

I want you to know the truth so you will discourage Mom from coming out here to spend her birthday with me. I know that's what she says she wants, but it's not a good idea. When I make my holiday call, none of this will be said, but you have to know that everyone here in Saw Hill knows, when strangers come, they're here to see us, and it isn't pleasant for them. For the same reason don't bother sending any packages. I'm telling Mom that we're forbidden to receive them, but the reason is that somehow by the time they get up here to us, most are empty or damaged. I got an empty Schrafft's candy box, probably from Lizzie and Mike. Don't tell Lizzie any of this. Don't even tell Jubal, because why make him worry? Now that I'm gone, you're the man of the family, Tommy, and the other thing is that I want you to know what to expect when it comes your time.

Nothing's hard about the day-to-day life, but it's boring and it's a lie to say we're doing work of national importance. They invent repairs we need to do on roads and trees to take down. They're just keeping us out of sight, and I suppose out of harm's way. Both Cal and I have put in for transfers someplace where we can at least help people. There are mental hospitals short of attendants, and there are some experimental medical programs needing volunteers.

Anything but this!

I worry a lot about Hope's brother, Abel. Hope says word is out that he's refusing to register for the draft, and that any day now he'll be arrested. Abel's always been a purist. He'll meet up with a lot of Jehovah's Witnesses in prison; there are more of them against registering than us. I've heard it's hard on all of them. I hate to think what the guards and even the other prisoners will do to a brilliant, sour character like him. But at least the horses will get a break with Abel gone.

You'll have some thinking to do, too, Tommy, in a short while, about what choice you'll make. That's why I'm going to keep you up-to-date on everything. Just you, brother. I don't want the family worried.

I pray for you and Jubal, Mom and Dad, Mahatma, and Quinn. Pray for me, too, and pray for peace.

Love,
Bud

P.S. Thanks for the sketches of Quinn. Do you ever think about becoming an artist?

★ ★ ★
SEVEN

YOUR SON IS YELLOW was the next graffito to appear on our store window, written in paint, and after that **BUD YELLOWBELLY!**

Dad hired a watchman, Slim Hislop. He sat overnight a few parking spaces from the store, in one of the trucks we used to haul merchandise to and from trains.

New Year's Eve was special to the Hislops; their kids came from all around. So that night I volunteered to fill in for him. Tommy said he'd keep me company because Lillie Light was at a Mennonite affair.

There was a big party at Wride Them Cowboy, all local merchants and their families invited. It was a restaurant in the heart of town, about four blocks from our store. All the waitresses dressed like cowgirls. Since the war most of them were older cowgirls. The younger ones were working for the other Wride, the onion man and Radio Dan's sponsor.

Tommy suggested we take turns looking in on it.

"Not me," I said. I was in blue jeans. "I'm not dressed for a party."

"You don't have to be dressed for Buck Wride's party!" Tommy said. But he was wearing the gray flannel pants and black turtleneck sweater Aunt Lizzie had given him from Santa. Before he'd mentioned the party, I'd wondered why he'd worn the long overcoat and the fedora to sit around in the front seat of a truck.

"If I was going to *any* party," I said, "I'd be going to the one at Friends School."

Even if I could have gone to that one, I doubted that I would have.

There'd be the same talk there always was in school, about how badly the war was going. Tommy said everything was turning around finally, and we were winning, and anyway at Sweet Creek High the kids tried not to dwell on our defeats—it wasn't good for morale. But at Friends most of the kids were Quakers. A lot of them felt these enormous guilt pangs about things like our troops surrendering to the Japs on Bataan, U-boats off the Atlantic coast sinking merchant ships headed for British ports, and the goose-steppers marching through Europe. Kids were debating what they'd do when they had to register for the draft, and a few were even questioning what right *anyone* had to be a conscientious objector in a war we could lose.

Since there was only one CO from Sweet Creek so far, the conversation usually got around to Bud. Nobody knocked him, not at SCFS, but some would ask me how he justified this, or that, and I'd tell them, "Ask him! I'm not him!"

Tommy said, "If you go to Wride's, you'll know plenty of people. Even Hope's going with Abel. Dad asked her, and she said yes."

"That's just who I'd like to see the New Year in with: Abel Hart!"

"He's not so bad, Jube. He's got a lot of guts not registering for the draft. He'll be going to prison . . . not jail, either: *prison*. For years!"

"He gives me the creeps, Tommy."

"A lot of visionaries are eccentric. But Abel's not going to be just a witness against the war—he's going to be a witness against the whole idea of conscription. Don't you think that takes guts?"

"I'm not sure anymore," I said. Before our country went to war, I was *so* sure. In school we'd recite the Litany of the War Resisters League: *If war comes, I will not fight. . . . If war comes, I will not enlist. . . . If war comes, I will not be conscripted. . . . If war comes, I will do nothing to support it. . . . If war comes, I will do everything to oppose it. . . . So help me God.*"

"I know how you feel," Tommy said. "You know what I did last week? You won't tell Mom and Dad?"

"No, of course not!"

"I bought some war stamps at school."

"I think Dad would understand. But Mom wouldn't," I said. "Did they make you buy them?"

"They don't *make* you, but they make a big thing out of it when you don't! Some kid'll say 'Maybe you should be back at SCFS, Tom. Maybe you miss hanging out with cowards.'"

"If they said that to me, the last thing I'd do is buy

the damn war stamps!"

"Sometimes I wonder if I should have transferred from Friends School," Tommy said. "All for basketball!"

Tommy took a pack of Camels out of his coat pocket, shook one up, and caught it between his lips. Then he scratched a match.

"Since when are you smoking?" I asked.

"A couple of months. Bud smokes too."

That was news to me. I said, "How does he afford it?" No one in a CPS camp was paid. The Society of Friends gave the COs $2.50 a month toward *all* their expenses, from toothpaste to underwear. German POWs in America received 80 cents a day for any work *they* did.

"Bud saved most of what he made at the Harts'," Tommy said. "But I don't think he's got that much, and he needs to see a dentist. If you ever want to do him a big favor, send him some cigarette money. Not the cigarettes, though. They'll get stolen."

"I remember when I used to know what my brothers were up to."

Tommy snickered. "Yeah, and you still do. I know you check out my graphs. And I know you read Bud's letter. I put a paper clip on top of it and shut that bottom drawer very carefully . . . and guess what wasn't there when I looked in my desk drawer next."

"Do you think I like being a sneak? It isn't fair, you know. I'll be fourteen in March."

"Fourteen!" Tommy exclaimed. "My my!"

Before he put out his cigarette, he blew a smoke ring, grinned at me, and said, "How's that?"

"Go on to the party," I said. "I know you don't want to sit here with your little thirteen-year-old brother on such a night as this!"

"You're right, little bro. On such a night as this, I need to find me a girl!"

"Good luck," I said.

I had a plan and a pocket flashlight to carry it out. I was going to begin reading what Natalia Granger said was the dirtiest book in the English language. It was called *God's Little Acre*, by Erskine Caldwell, and it had arrived that afternoon (in exchange for Tommy's socks) complete with the "good parts" marked by paper clips.

It was set in Georgia, and the characters had names like Ty Ty and Darling Jill.

I read the "good parts" first—there were plenty of them. I'd look up and watch the store in between hot passages. There was a light snowfall beginning. Pilgrim Lane was quiet. It always was around ten at night, and New Year's Eve was no exception.

When I'd finished all the good parts, I went back to the beginning. It was an easy read, and I got right into it. I got way into it. When I remembered what I was there for, the culprit had already started to paint a yellow stripe across the store window.

I shoved the paperback book into my pocket and very

carefully opened the door of the truck. When my feet touched the ground, I reached behind the driver's seat for the lariat Tommy and I had put there. Last summer Bud had taught Tommy and me how to lasso. Some of the horses at the Harts' were tamed, trained, then sold to the Mennonites to drive their buggies. We had to know how to catch and tame them.

I shut the door quietly and went toward the fellow in a crouch, holding the rope, my heart pounding because I'd never tethered a person. He was moving fast, leaving the paint can behind him, running the brush in a long yellow line.

I figured I could handle him easily once I had him. He was smaller than me, thinner, too. He had a wool cap on, and a red-and-black mackinaw jacket.

I swung the rope.

"Gotcha!" I called out. I'd pinned his arms, and I pulled hard.

Then, as he dropped the paintbrush and tried to move his arms some way that would budge the rope, I got myself over to the door. I slammed my weight against it and triggered the alarm.

The siren sounded. Burglar alarms in Sweet Creek had to sound like loud duck calls, so as not to be confused with a fire alarm or an air-raid alarm.

But the police would know there was trouble at E. F. Shoemaker's.

"Damn you! Why'd you call the police?"

He sounded like a kid, like someone younger than

me, and I started walking toward him. "Did you think you were going to get away with it?"

"I'm going to catch hell unless you get me out of here! Get me out of here, Jubal!"

"Who's talking?" I couldn't see the face under the cap.

"Take the cap off, why don't you?"

So he wouldn't try any tricks, I sprang forward and grabbed it, then jumped back.

The brown hair spilled down to her shoulders, and her mouth tipped in a snide grin. "You roped in a girl, Jubal! Get me out of here!"

"Darie Daniel?"

"The police are going to be here any minute, Jubal Shoemaker! I'll never, ever forgive you if you get me in trouble!"

"You got *yourself* in trouble!"

"Then get me out! I'm tied up like an animal, for Pete's sake! JUBAL?"

I was already on my way to her.

★ ★ ★

EIGHT

That was the beginning of my fascination with Daria
Daniel. I was the only one who never called her Darie.
I vowed that I wouldn't that first night we met, after
we hurried away from the police and the paint bucket and
the yellow stripe on our store window. We went to The
Sweet Creek Diner, where she ordered a coffee and I
ordered a Coke.

"Never call me Darie," she said. "Promise? I'm trying
to outgrow that name."

"I promise."

What was I doing promising her *anything*? My
loyalties should have been with my big brother, not
her. My eyes and my mouth weren't paying any attention to my thoughts.

"My father's real name is Lucio Danelli. I can understand why he changed Lucio to Dan, because kids called
him Lucy, but why did he let my mother talk him into
changing our name to Daniel?"

"Did she ever give you a reason?" I asked her.

"Yes. She claims it's best not to be too much of one
thing. Don't be too Italian or too Jewish or too Irish."
Her eyes looked directly at me. "Or too Quaker," she
said.

★ 54 ★

Oh, great! I thought, just great. I said, "How about too Catholic?"

"Same thing." She shrugged. "My mother's nothing. She's Protestant or something. Now she goes to St. Peter's most Sundays because of the war."

After the waitress brought our order, I looked across at Daria, wondering why I was afraid to ask the question I was about to ask, wondering what there was about her that made me want her to like me. She was about my age, I knew, but I always felt a lot younger around her, and I didn't have a reason for that either.

She was putting heaping teaspoons of sugar in her coffee, her brown hair touching her shoulders, the checkered cap cocked over one eye.

"Daria, why would you mark my father's windows? Do you think my father had anything to do with Bud becoming a CO?"

"I don't know." She looked up at me with these sea-green eyes of hers. She was blinking as though *I* made *her* nervous. That was a laugh. She said, "My mother says your father was never really religious before he met your mother."

"He's not really religious now."

"I guess the most religious person in your family is Bud."

"My mother, and then Bud. . . . Then me."

"Are you really?"

"I'm not passionately religious. Sometimes I envy people who are. But I believe in God. And I think I feel strongly about what's right and what's wrong."

"I'm not that religious," she said, "but since the war, I go to church every Sunday like my mother."

"Who put you up to painting our window, Daria? Radio Dan?"

"*Daddy?* Oh, my gawd, you don't know Daddy!"

"Just what I hear over the radio. You're not supposed to clap your hands until the war's over. You can only slap your sides."

"I wouldn't think *you'd* listen."

"I don't always listen."

"Daddy doesn't like to make enemies, not even of slackers."

"Don't call my brother a slacker! You don't know anything about him!"

"I know he's letting my two brothers fight for this country, when *he* won't."

"What Bud is doing is for this country," I said. "He's trying to stop sending guys like your brother off to war!"

"But that won't stop Hitler! How do you stop Hitler?"

"I don't know," I said. Even kids at Friends admitted Hitler was a different kind of enemy.

"It was my idea to mark the windows, Jubal! It's the least I can do, with both my brothers risking their lives. Let me ask you something, Jubal. Suppose there was a mad dog loose on our street, foaming at the mouth, his ruff up, his teeth bared as he went after people. Would Bud just walk away and leave it up to my brothers to make the neighborhood safe again?"

"There aren't any dogs involved, Daria. Just human beings like us."

"Why should Danny Jr. and Dean have to fight them and not Bud? "

"Because Bud doesn't agree with our government that the only way to stop madness is to become mad yourself."

She sighed and shook her head. Finally she said, "Jubal? Let's not talk about this. You can report me to the police—I don't care. But let's you and me just be friends, and leave the war out of it."

"Sounds good to me."

"Me too."

I told her I wouldn't tell on her if she'd vow not to go near the store window again. She said she wouldn't, because she thought she really liked me. I *knew* I really liked her.

I showed her the Caldwell book and told her about my cousin Natalia, and she said she would rather live in Greenwich Village than anyplace in the world because a poet named Edna St. Vincent Millay had lived there.

"I suppose *you* don't know her," she teased.

"I'm not a big reader anymore. I don't have time." I explained that several afternoons a week I helped out at the Hart farm, and I worked all day there on Saturdays.

"I see," she said. "You have time to read dirty parts of books, but not things like "'O world, I cannot hold thee close enough!'"

"Hold *thee* close enough?"

"Hold thee close enough."

"Why does she say hold *thee* close enough?"

"Not because she's one of you Quakers, if that's what you think. It's just poetic."

She looked at her watch. "I have to go. I said I'd be home by midnight. My parents think I'm at the Sweet Creek High party."

"In those clothes?"

"It was a masquerade," she said. "Come as someone you admire."

She wore the plaid mackinaw over her shoulders and under it Danny Jr.'s green-and-white letter sweater, won when he was SCHS's star quarterback. Her jeans were rolled at the cuffs, and she had on black boots.

"Then you're supposed to be Danny Jr.?"

"I'd rather go to a party as my favorite brother than be at Wride Them Cowboy. Who wants to spend New Year's Eve with your parents' friends?" Her feet were keeping time with the song on the jukebox, "Be Careful, It's My Heart."

She suddenly sang out, "*It's not the ground you walk on, it's my heart.*"

"You have a nice voice," I said.

"Thanks to Mrs. Ochevsky, my singing teacher."

"Why, she lives right next door to the Harts, in Doylestown."

"Sometimes I see the horses, and I wish I could ride again. I used to ride at Luke Casper's, with Danny Jr., but I had to choose between riding lessons and voice lessons. Mrs. Ochevsky won out. I'd like to sing with a band someday."

"You sound swell, so you should be able to do it."

Daria leaned down and blew away some spilled sugar. Then she stood and asked me if I was going home. We didn't live that far away from each other.

"I'm not going home yet. I'm supposed to be guarding the store."

"I remember when I used to shop at your store, you were there sometimes. Were you working there?"

"Ever since I can remember. There was always something for me to do."

"What needs to be done in that store is paint the walls."

"Paint the walls?"

She nodded.

"They were just painted last spring," I said. Marty Allen, my best friend, had helped Bud and me do the job. Tommy was always at basketball practice.

"I hate the color of the walls in your store. They remind me of upchuck. Your father should paint everything white."

"I'll tell him."

"I never meant to hurt your dad, Jubal."

"But you did. I have to tell you that you did."

"I get so angry sometimes. Not really at your dad. But at my brothers just being swooped up and sent to war," she said.

I didn't point out that Danny Jr. hadn't been swooped

up, that he'd volunteered when he was seventeen. Dean waited until he was draft age to enlist.

If we were going to be friends, there were a lot of things I wouldn't be pointing out and vice versa.

I helped her get her arms into her coat sleeves.

There was a light snow still falling outside the diner.

"Happy 1943, Jubal."

I wanted to say that I hoped she'd be a big part of it.

But "Yes" was all I could manage. And "Happy New Year, Daria."

★ ★ ★
NINE

hen I got back to Pilgrim Lane, the police were just pulling away. There was a smear where the yellow stripe had been. My father smelled of turpentine.

"Where were you, Jubal? I was worried about you."

"I lassoed the guy, but he got away."

"We saw the rope . . . and the paint can. The police took the paint can for evidence."

"What? Fingerprints or something?"

"Well, they'll likely ask at Hampton Hardware if anyone can remember someone buying that particular paint."

"Okay." Daria told me it was an old can from her family's cellar, so I felt relieved that probably nothing was going to be found out about who did it.

"But where *were* you, Jubal?" My father had on the heavy gray sweater Aunt Lizzie had given him for Christmas. He was looking down at me with a frown, the snow on his thick black hair.

"I got winded chasing him," I told him. "I went into the diner to see if anyone had seen him around. I got a Coke."

"What'd he look like? Was he a boy or a man?"

"I couldn't see his face. He had a stocking cap pulled down to his eyes, and he had a scarf around his neck. A red scarf. He wasn't a big guy. I'm taller."

I had never lied to my father before, and I was surprised that what I was telling him came from me easily and seemed like a game.

My father shook his head. "I wish I knew who was doing it."

I would have liked to tell him that it was just Daria Daniel, no big deal, because once I knew it was her, I felt relieved. I didn't figure her as much of an enemy, and she was only a girl, too. But I wasn't sure how he'd take it: whether he'd tell Radio Dan and get Daria in trouble, or just walk around sadly the way he had last Sunday morning, as though someone had betrayed him. Neither thing was good.

On the way home he told me that he and Hope, Abel, and Tommy had left Wride Them Cowboy early.

"I should never have taken them there with me," he said. "When your mother refused to go, I thought I ought to show up because I'm in Rotary with Dan. I'd just look in, I thought. . . . Someone spiked Abel's punch. There must have been a lot of alcohol in it, because he's been throwing up like a poisoned dog."

"Just Abel's punch?"

"Word's around he's not registering for the draft, that's why."

"Are you sure that's why?"

"I've heard talk of it at Rotary, too. . . . But I can't help feeling sorry for the boy. I never saw anyone vomit like that."

"You know what, Dad? We ought to paint the store. Not the outside but inside. We ought to paint the walls white."

"What made you think of that suddenly?"

"I don't know."

"You're right. I don't like the pale yellow. There's a project for you and your pal Marty Allen in the new year."

"When I can get to it. Tommy and I have our hands full at the Harts'."

"And now you're losing Abel."

"He was never any help, Dad."

The Sweet Creek Savings Bank clock chimed, and Dad said, "This will be the first time we begin a new year without Bud."

"Dad?"

"What, son?"

"Would you have done what Bud did?"

"I've thought a lot about that, as you can imagine. . . . I just don't know."

"At Friends kids say this war is different. Someone I know asked me if there's a rabid dog in the neighborhood, shouldn't you help kill it so the neighborhood's safe?"

Dad said, "Jubal, you can't equate killing a mad dog with dropping tons of bombs on innocent civilians."

"But even some guys at school are saying they aren't going to be COs."

"It takes confidence and conviction to witness, Jubal. There aren't many like your brother."

We rode along awhile before Dad said, "Guess who

bought a double-layer chocolate cake with a fudge frost-
ing, and put it in our refrigerator."

"Not Hope?" I thought he was heading in that direction because he had this little grin. Hope was known to
be a tightwad.

"That's who," he said. "She says she's got an announcement."

"Uh-oh," I said. "Is Bud going to marry her?"

"I hope not."

"I hope not too."

"She's all right," Dad hurried to add.

It was snowing harder. In the houses we passed, we
could see the Christmas-tree lights. Everything looked
like the inside of one of those snow globes. . . . I was
thinking, If Bud marries Hope, that drip Abel will be my
brother-in-law.

Just as we pulled into our driveway, the town siren
was sounding and church bells were ringing.

Abel Hart with his fire-red hair was sitting at our
kitchen table, sipping hot cocoa, his face white as flour.
I didn't say anything to him, and he didn't say anything
to me. Tommy had one of those little horns to his lips
that unrolled a snake of red tissue when you blew it.

Everybody was wishing everybody Happy New Year,
and even Mahatma was smiling and wagging his tail, a
big red bow around his neck.

Mom was torn between smiling and not, still a
Quaker to her bones.

If her heart wasn't in featuring the first day of 1943,

it *was* in all of us being together as a family.

Finally, Hope brought out the cake.

"I've got an announcement," Hope said.

We were all standing around in the kitchen for some reason, and suddenly it got quiet and all eyes were on Hope.

"Maybe you know the American Friends Service Committee sponsors an all-women CPS Unit. I've accepted a job at a CPS camp in Virginia as the dietitian."

"Oh, Hope!" my mother exclaimed, and everyone began to clap.

I was really clapping, and when I looked over at Dad, he was too, all smiles.

★ ★ ★

PART TWO

★ ★ ★

Listeners, before we say good night, I want to read you something that will break your hearts. I found it when I opened my copy of Life magazine this morning. It happens to be an advertisement for the New Haven Railroad, but don't hold that against it.

What you see is this kid in the upper berth of a train, and here goes with the copy:

Tonight he knows he is leaving behind a lot of little things—and big ones.

The taste of hamburgers and pop . . . the feel of driving a roadster over a six-lane highway . . . a dog named Shucks, or Spot, or Barnacle Bill. The pretty girl who writes so often . . . that gray-haired man so proud and awkward at the station . . . the mother who knits the socks he'll wear soon.

Tonight he's thinking them over.

There's a lump in his throat . . . and maybe a tear fills his eye.

It doesn't matter, kid. Nobody will see. It's too dark.

Listeners, time out. I've got a lump in my own throat, and a tear in my eye too. . . . I think you can take a look at your own copy of Life and read it to the end.

Say a prayer for our boys wherever they may be. Pray that one day we can clap our hands again, that we will have won the war and our boys will be on their way back home for keeps.

My daughter, Darie, the only child I have left at home, now that my twin sons are fighting for their Uncle Sam, will sing us out as usual.

> If your boy is in the Army, slap your sides,
> If your boy is in the Navy, slap your sides,
> If your boy's in the Marines,
>   and you know what V-mail means,
> Slap your sides,
> Slap for Wride's,
> Slap your sides!

—<u>Radio Dan broadcast, 1943</u>

★ ★ ★

TEN

That February I got a letter from Natalia telling me she'd send me a book called *A Tree Grows in Brooklyn*, with one "really good part" in it, if I would send her a picture of Tommy.

I didn't read that part aloud at dinner, but I read the P.S. that said Freud had died and my Aunt Lizzie was "devastated."

"Oh, dear, I'll have to call her tonight," Mom said.

"Devastated about a cat's death!" My father pushed his chair back from the table.

"Well don't we feel terrible about Quinn?" my mother said.

"What about Quinn?" Dad grumbled.

"Haven't you paid any attention to what Tommy and Jubal have been talking about? That horse just can't get over Bud's absence."

"Oh, dear me," my father said sarcastically.

This was the winter of their discontent, as Shakespeare might have put it, a time when they couldn't agree on anything. When Dad took my advice and helped me paint the store walls white, Mom said the house trim needed it more. When Bud got transferred to a volunteer job in a mental hospital, Mom wept, fearful for him, but

Dad said he'd be of more use there than off in the woods felling trees.

Dad had made a little den for himself downstairs in the basement, where he read the papers and now listened to the radio, too: Lowell Thomas, Gabriel Heatter, even Radio Dan (Listeners, Ginny Rippon wants to share a letter from hubby, who's flying missions over Germany, and begins, *Darling, I think of you as we go through the darkness on a starry night, carrying our killer bombload to Kraut targets*). I'd hear Daria singing "Slap Your Sides."

Dad also followed the war with an atlas by the armchair he'd moved there. On a map of North Africa he'd marked a spot with a pin and written "Kasserine Pass. 1st defeat of Americans at the hands of Germans!"

My parents were not sharing the same bedroom anymore either. Mom blamed it on Dad's snoring, but he had always snored, and all of us had always slept through it.

Then word came that one afternoon the doorbell rang at Judge Edward Whipple's, and old Mr. Chayka delivered one of those telegrams with stars on the envelope. Eddie Jr.'s plane had not come back from a mission over Germany.

A few days later my father came home with an armband and an air-raid warden's helmet. He refused to discuss his new role as a neighborhood volunteer with anyone in the family. The fact was, no one asked him about it.

It was a dreary February, with rotten weather to go

with news of more servicemen's lives lost, thousands of people dying or becoming crippled from polio, and everything rationed from shoes to butter to canned goods. Ever since Daria had marked the store windows, someone copied her three times, not bothering with words, just a large yellow Y.

On the one-thirty bus I took to Doylestown, to work at the Harts', there sat Daria one Saturday. I'd run into her in Sweet Creek three times since New Year's Eve, but she was always with one of her parents.

That day she was going to Mrs. Ochevsky's for her singing lesson. She greeted me with a big smile.

"My mother always drove me, but she says we can't use our gas rationing tickets for recreational things anymore," she said.

"That's a little insulting, since you're pursuing a career as a professional singer."

She gave me a surprised look. "I'm amazed you remembered that about me."

Then she asked me what it was, exactly, that I did at the Harts'.

"You probably told me before, but—" She didn't finish her sentence.

"But you didn't listen."

"Am I supposed to hang on your every word?"

I felt like saying, Why *not*? I hang on *yours*.

She was in that same plaid mackinaw that was too big for her, blue jeans, and boots. Her ears were covered with furry red earmuffs. Nobody would ever call her a beauty, but there was something about her that stopped me cold. I'd be looking straight ahead all the while I was sneaking peeks of her out of the corner of my eye.

I told her what I did at the Harts'. "I take over for Tommy and Luke Casper, who've been there since early morning. I muck out the stalls, feed the horses, exercise them, whatever has to be done."

"Oh, how I'd love to ride one!"

"Well, you can. Just come over after your lesson."

"Are you kidding me, Jubal Shoemaker?"

My heart was pounding. "Show up and see," I said.

Tommy was sketching Quinn through the barn window. "Look at him out there," he said. "What a sad sack! First his owner has to board him, then Bud disappears. This morning Mr. Hart told me Quinn was *bereaved*. He said, 'That makes two of us, Tom. Quinn and yours truly.' Then he read me parts of a letter from Abel. He's in Florida, some prison in Tallahassee, and he's already in trouble."

"Surprise, surprise," I said.

"You don't get him. He tries to do the right thing, but it always backfires on him," Tommy said. "First he tried to eat with the Negro prisoners because he's against segregation, and they put him in isolation for that. Next he got put in for writing letters for the Negroes. He says more prisoners there are illiterate than literate, so he was helping everyone he could. It was okay for him to help whites, but not the Negroes."

"It's a southern prison. What did he expect?" I said.

"That's not very sympathetic, Jube." Tommy put the crayon in his pocket and closed his sketchbook.

"Well, he thinks he can change the world single-handed, and overnight, too. Bud always said that kind of crusader is more nuts than principled."

"Bud admires Abel, didn't you know that?"

"Okay, but I'm not Bud."

"You ought to figure out why Abel gets under your skin."

"Because a lot of people think that's what a Quaker is."

"So what?"

"Don't *you* lecture me, Tommy! You didn't stick it out at Friends! You don't have any idea what it's like to be a Quaker around here now!"

"I know what it's like, little bro. Just because I'm at SCHS doesn't mean I'm not thought of as a Quaker. . . . But no one thinks I'm like Abel, either. Everyone knows he's eccentric."

"I don't wish him harm," I said. I didn't.

Behind Tommy, in the paddock, Quinn was standing with his head down and his tail dropped. He looked thinner. So did Mr. Hart, who was riding the tractor around to push snow away from the pasture. He had red hair too, and that same really white complexion, but somehow he didn't look weird like Abel. Just ordinary, just plain, the way he wanted to be thought of: Quaker plain.

"This is for you to read and keep to yourself," said

Tommy. He passed me a letter with Bud's writing on the envelope, and the same PERSONAL printed on both sides in big letters and underlined.

"How's he doing?"

"You'll see," Tommy said. "Quinn could use some exercise, but he doesn't seem to want anyone on him today. Luke Casper tried. So did I."

I wasn't keen about riding Quinn when he was depressed. Sometimes his mood bordered on anger. I'd seen him throw both Luke and Mr. Hart. Deliberately. I'd probably walk him around by his lunge rein for a while.

Tommy had already mucked out, so I went in to see Baby Boy and Heavenly. They'd been exercised by Tommy and they were in good shape.

I took time out to read Bud's letter.

He was part of a CPS unit that had been transferred to Shenandoah State Asylum for the Insane, near Staunton, Virginia.

Dear Tommy and Jubal,

The only good thing about this assignment is that occasionally I'll be able to see Hope. At least we're in the same state.

This place is a bedlam where the attendants treat the patients like animals. Some patients don't even wear clothes; they lie about on filthy floors in their own urine and feces, their meals shoved at them on tin plates, no silver, and they all drink from the same wall faucet turned on for fire drills or to hose down the place.

I can't begin to describe it all, and I wouldn't if I had time because words couldn't do justice to this living hell! We work 12-hour shifts, and there are only 100 attendants to care for 3,500 male patients. 16 of the attendants are COs, and we are not liked by the other workers, who won't sit with us "lily-livers" in the dining room. . . . You have to have a tough hide down here. I get Tuesday night off, so I went into Shenandoah Village to see a movie, any movie at this point because I haven't been to one in a year! Just as I'm about to pass my money to the cashier, I see this sign pasted to her window:

NO SKUNKS ALLOWED!
SO YOU CONSCIENTIOUS OBJECTORS
STAY THE HELL AWAY FROM
THIS THEATER!

I found out there are signs like that in a lot of the stores, because they know we're working at the hospital. There was even an editorial in the local newspaper stating that "while the citizens of Shenandoah Village are buying war bonds in greater numbers than ever before, how many are 'Hitler's pals' volunteering at the insane asylum buying? The answer is zero! They know who to help out and who not to, it seems."

Still, rumor has it that a new director on his way here is a good guy, so we put our hope halfway on him, and the other half on our own determination and resourcefulness to work a miracle here . . . somehow.

How is Quinn doing? Are you giving him molasses treats? Is Luke Casper drinking around him? I hope not. Quinn hates that smell, or maybe he senses, when he smells it, that Luke might treat him roughly. And old Mahatma, how's he? I know you all can get along without me just fine, so I guess I have to invent the notion that my critters miss me.

I think I understand what Dad is going through. For one thing he was never a heartfelt Quaker, never that religious . . . but for another, unlike Mom, he has to go out into the community every day and mingle with men who have sons in the service and sit through those stupid Rotary lunches every Tuesday. Dad's never had a defiant spirit, and anyway this should be *my* problem, not his! I hope there's no more stuff going on with the store windows!

I get letters from Lizzie, each one shorter than the last, until finally there's no hello or good-bye, just something like "The Jews of France are all in concentration camps!" . . . "Kiss the Jews of Greece good-bye!"

You both have to think hard about how much you can bear before you decide what position you're going to take. We have some COs who've already chickened out and put in for 1AOs, and they're in the army now. But more stick to their convictions, and I've never associated with finer men.

Mom is still threatening to visit me for her birthday. I don't want her to see this place, or visit any town near a CPS camp. I'm toying with the idea of taking a furlough in the spring, which might satisfy her. I'd meet her in New York City, since it would just embarrass Dad if I came home. She could see Lizzie then, too.

I miss you all and I pray for you, and for peace.

Love,
Bud

I had just finished the letter when I heard Quinn whinny out in the paddock.

I came out of the barn to see Daria talking to him, all the while stroking his neck and giving him cubes of sugar.

I went down there, and as I came toward her, she said,

"Just talk to me in a natural voice now, Jubal, because this horse is stressed."

"How did you know that?"

"Both Luke and Danny Jr. taught me a lot about horses. While I was warming up with scales, I was watching this one from Mrs. Ochevsky's window. He looks so unhappy."

"He is."

"He's beautiful," she said. She was patting him firmly on the neck and shoulders. She knew enough not to pat his nose. Most horses didn't like it.

"He's Bud's favorite," I told her. "Bud says he's extra intelligent."

"And sensitive," Daria said. "Well, at least Bud's right about something. What's his name?"

"Quinn."

"I got sugar from Mrs. Ochevsky. Do you think I could ride him?"

"If he'll let you."

"Just keep talking to me. Just say nice things to me."

"Did you notice we painted the walls of the store white?" I said.

"Why would I notice that?"

"Because you suggested it. Don't you remember? You told me New Year's Eve the yellow walls looked like puke."

"I'd never say that word," she said. "I hate crass words."

I couldn't believe the way Quinn was taking to her,

putting his nose right down in her coat collar, his tail lifting.

After a while we walked him back to the tack room in the barn.

I had an idea Quinn was going to let her ride him.

When we came back out with him saddled, Daria got on him easily. Quinn's ears didn't move, a good sign. He shook his head the way some horses do when spring comes, to shake out the winter kinks.

Quinn was a goner from the time she sat on him. He pranced, snorted, danced, and I swear he grinned, too.

I went across to the fence and opened it for them.

★ ★ ★
ELEVEN

Daria came to ride Quinn every Saturday after that. When we'd come back from Doylestown on the bus together, she always wanted to go to The Sweet Creek Diner. She said it was our hangout. Even though I didn't like coffee very much, I always ordered a cup, as she did.

"Italian is my favorite language" was the kind of pronouncement she would make, and sometimes, very quietly, she would sing something from an opera. *"Non mi dir . . ." "O don fatale . . ." "D'amore al dolce impero."*

I, who didn't know bull about classical music, soon knew to request the song from Mozart's *Don Giovanni*, from Verdi's *Don Carlo*, from Rossini's *Armida*.

"I don't really want to be an opera star," Daria told me, "but Mrs. Ochevsky says it's the best training for my instrument, and it's also the way I learn Italian."

"What instrument do you play?" I asked her.

"Oh, Jubal, you're so young, aren't you? My instrument is my voice."

"I see."

"Now your feelings are hurt," she said. "I'm sorry, Jubal."

"You could just tell me your voice is your instrument without telling me I'm so young. I'm the same age you are, Daria!"

"It's not your fault. Boys don't mature as quickly as girls do."

I was changing because of her. She was about an inch taller than I was, so I began measuring myself. Everywhere! I was looking in the mirror more. And I put a few drops of Tommy's Vitalis on my hair. Sometimes I borrowed his clothes: a sweater, a scarf.

Once he remarked that he had an idea I'd been helping myself for a while now, and when I swore it wasn't true, he said his favorite socks were missing. The brown-and-white-checked ones. He knew they were somewhere in my drawers, but he wasn't going to search them just to prove I was a liar.

"I'm not!" I said.

"There's such a thing as lying by omission. For instance, you never told me you sent Aunt Lizzie the picture of me from *The Sweet Creek Citizen*. The other night on the phone she told Mom she was real proud of me being a basketball star!"

Then I confessed that Natalia had a crush on him, had the socks, and had been sent the photo. "She sent me a book called *God's Little Acre* for the socks, and *The Fountainhead* for the picture."

"I wondered what'd happened to your reading tastes."

Daria complained about those books, too, when I told her about them. "I don't have anything against sexy stuff," she said. "I like sexy stuff, but you're reading the whole book!"

She said in a few years I would be an embarrassment to myself because I wasn't worldly or sensitive.

She said Danny Jr., even off somewhere in the jungle, could still find Browning, Conrad, Frost, Homer, Tennyson, and Wordsworth, just to name a few of the books he read.

"*You* send them to him," I said.

"Sometimes. Sometimes he gets them from his buddies. They pool what they have. Of course, Danny Jr. gets his pick of the good books, because nobody else wants those. Most of the men like westerns or thrillers or even comic books."

"But not dear old Danny Jr.," I said sarcastically.

"No, not dear old Danny Jr., Jubal, and your whole face looks just awful when you smirk that way."

I think she knew I was jealous of Danny Jr., and she rubbed it in the way another girl might praise a boyfriend while some poor dope was trying to impress her.

It wasn't easy to impress Daria. When she'd asked me what I wanted to do with my life, I'd told her I'd probably go someplace Quaker like Swarthmore or Haverford, then after college return to work with Dad.

"He says his dream is to have Shoemaker & Sons on the window someday," I'd said.

"Do you and your brothers want to run a department store?" She'd sounded as though she was asking me if we wanted to be garbagemen.

"Why not?"

"Even Bud?"

"Maybe. What about Danny Jr.? What's he going to do?"

"He doesn't want us to call him Junior anymore, either."

"What'll Danny do?"

"He's going to be a famous writer," Daria'd said.

On this particular afternoon, there seemed to be more servicemen than ever in the diner. A lot of them were fellows home on leave or furlough, but some were stationed nearby. They came to Sweet Creek to see movies or to visit the Side Door Canteen, in the basement of City Hall.

The songs playing on the jukebox were the usual: "You'd Be So Nice to Come Home to, " "Don't Get Around Much Anymore," "When the Lights Go On Again All Over the World," on and on.

Sometimes you can tell when someone's thinking the very same thing you are. I wasn't surprised when Daria looked across at me and said, "Does it make you uncomfortable that *everything* is about the war?"

"Why should it?" But I couldn't look her in the eye.

"Do you know what you'll do if it's still going on when you're draft age?"

"I know what I hope I have the courage to do."

"I suppose you're going to try and tell me you need courage to be a coward."

"I'm not going to try and tell you *anything*."

"Good, because I don't need to hear it."

She was silent for a while, and then she said, "Don't you realize that the whole country can't be wrong? *Everyone* is doing their bit. Even some Japanese Americans are, when they have every reason to hate us for putting their relatives in internment camps! I'm doing this paper for school," she said. "It's about this Japanese American unit training at Camp Shelby in Mississippi."

"I read about them," I said. Lizzie'd sent Mom an article from the *New York Journal-American* about Negroes who had their own unit, and Japs who did. She'd written across the top, *Show this to Tommy and Jubal. Ask them if they're content to let the colored and the Japs fight our war for them.*

Daria said, "Where did you read about them? I have just this little United Press release from *The Citizen*."

When I told her about the newspaper article my aunt had sent, Daria said she'd give anything to read it.

"I'll bring it over tonight," I said. "Do you ever listen to 'Your Hit Parade'?"

"Couldn't you just slip it in our mailbox?" she asked.

"Sure, I could. But do you ever listen to 'Your Hit Parade'? I listen to it sometimes." I listened to it a lot less since the songs became all about the war.

"I always listen to it," Daria said, "but it's not a good idea for you to come over tonight."

"Why is that?"

"It just isn't."

"You're going to listen to it with someone?"

"I'm going to listen to it with my mother."

She was putting her mackinaw on and flipping a red scarf over her shoulder.

"Wouldn't you rather listen to it with me?"

"Maybe I would, Jubal," she said, "but I can't." She was on her feet, and I was too. Behind her there was a poster of a dead paratrooper's body settling to earth, his head hanging, eyes shut, his toes just starting to drag across the ground. There was blood on his jacket and his hand. Underneath the drawing of him were the words: **CARELESS TALK GOT THERE FIRST.**

Daria waited until we got outside.

"Jubal, don't you ever wonder why I want to come here when we get back from Doylestown? We don't live that far away from each other, and I make much better coffee."

"I just thought . . . I thought it was more private than right under your parents' noses. I thought—"

She cut me off, speaking very fast. "Daddy doesn't think it's good for me to be around you people too much," she said.

"You mean the Shoemakers? Is that what you mean?"

"He likes your mom and your dad, and he'd probably like you and Tommy too, but Bud is another matter. Bud has changed things, Jubal. A lot of people don't like what he's done. It's not just us!"

"I know that!"

"I even feel guilty about my Saturdays with you at the

Harts'. Hope Hart is planning meals for conscientious objectors! And then there's Abel. Abel is breaking the law"—she waved her hand like a wand—"just ignoring the draft!"

"He's a very orthodox Quaker, Daria." I never thought I'd defend Abel.

"He's a traitor, Jubal! One of the finest things I ever did in my entire life was to mark your store windows! For once *I* was doing something about the war! I wasn't being careful or being discreet because of Daddy! I should have kept right on!"

"I'm glad you didn't. It's my father you were hurting, not Bud."

"Now Daddy says it isn't good business for me to fraternize with you. He thinks I run into you on the bus and we talk. He would hate it that I meet you at the Harts', that we go for coffee after!"

I don't remember what we talked about the rest of the way home. She was good at babbling. She was also liable to burst into a few bars of song, and I remember that day it was "As Time Goes By," which was from the movie *Casablanca*. Tommy and I had gone to it together, and afterward Tommy kept imitating Humphrey Bogart saying, "Here's lookin' at you, kid!"

I was quiet, letting it slowly sink in that in Radio Dan's view, our hanging out together wasn't very different from certain French people "fraternizing" with the Germans. I'd first heard that word watching a "March of Time" newsreel. They'd shown villagers someplace outside Paris shaving a woman's head because she'd been with a Nazi.

When we got to Daria's house, I noticed for the first time that she gave a quick wave and a "'Bye," and hurried down the driveway. It was dark out by then. The Daniels' porch lights were on, but she always went in the side door. I decided that was so she could sneak in, and so they wouldn't look out the windows and see me walking away from the house.

★ ★ ★

TWELVE

I was still mulling over the idea of Daria "fraternizing" with me when I got home.

Mom looked happier than I'd seen her look in months.

"Guess what, Jubal! Tommy and you and I are going to New York City in April. Tommy will have time off for Easter vacation, and Friends will be on spring recess. We can stay with Lizzie."

"Great!" I said. "Was it Lizzie's idea?"

"Bud thought of it. He's taking a furlough to work with Dorothy Day for two weeks."

"Who's Dorothy Day?"

"She's a Catholic pacifist who runs soup kitchens for the poor in lower Manhattan. Bud doesn't want to stay with Lizzie."

My father opened the door from the basement, walked across to the staircase, and went up without a word.

"I don't know what's wrong with him anymore, Jubal," said Mom.

"Sure you do, Mom. Start with the yellow Y that appears on the windows from time to time, and the customers who don't come in anymore."

"Are you sure about customers not coming in any-more?"

"Well, a few aren't." I tried to soften it. I'd forgotten how Dad always kept bad news to himself.

I gave Mom a kiss and got Mahatma's leash from the closet. When he saw me with it, he began walking around, wagging his tail and rattling his dog tags.

I went upstairs and got the *Journal-American* article from my desk, put it in an envelope, and scrawled Daria's name across it. When I went down to the bathroom, Dad was sitting on the side of the tub, waiting for it to fill.

"Take your coat off and stay awhile," he said.

"I'm taking Mahatma for a walk."

"What has your mother got to say about me?"

"Nothing," I said.

"I bet," he said.

After I zipped up, I got a look at dad naked. I hadn't seen him without clothes since summer. He was getting a paunch. Flab under his arms, too. I was surprised. I couldn't imagine that he didn't still work out at the Y. Then wasn't the time to ask him.

I took a flashlight and walked down to the Daniels' with Mahatma.

Their mailbox was all the way up on their porch. The front hall window had the flag with two blue stars on it, one for Dean and one for Danny. I stuck the article inside and sneaked a look through the living-room curtains. Mrs. Daniel was playing the piano, and Daria was stand-ing facing her, singing. I couldn't make out the song.

"She's got an instrument," I told Mahatma as we headed back down the street.

Later that night she called me. She told me, "What I said doesn't mean we can't be together, Quinn."

"Did you hear what you just called me?" I asked her.

"I did it on purpose."

"I don't believe you, Daria."

"Why? Can't you believe I'd miss you?"

She hung up before I could answer.

★ ★ ★

THIRTEEN

Our first day in New York, Bud invited Tommy and me to lunch: "just us three," and he gave us subway directions to the lower east side.

There were some bums sleeping it off in front of the building that housed the soup kitchen. There were more inside who smelled of booze, weren't shaved, looked like they'd worn the clothes they had on for a year.

I could tell Tommy was as uneasy as I was. Neither of us had ever seen anything like it. In Sweet Creek we had one town drunk who slept outside the railroad station. People left old coats and gloves for him.

"There're even some *women* here," Tommy said. He was all dressed up in his best glen plaid double-breasted suit, shoes shined, clean white shirt, black knit tie.

Bud was coming toward us in shirtsleeves, all grins. "Where are you two going, to a dance?"

I wasn't that dressed up, but I did have on a suit and tie.

"Follow me," said Bud, leading us down a staircase to the basement.

There were long tables in rows. There was a low roar of voices, and the sounds of chairs being pushed on the bare floors. I'd never seen or smelled people like that.

"Let's grab some plates," Bud said.

"We're eating here?" I said.

"We're in luck, because it's a chili day."

We followed him down to the food line while he told us he was sorry we couldn't meet Dorothy Day, the Catholic pacifist who'd founded the shelter. She was off at a CPS camp.

"She helps the guys' morale with her visits," he said. "Even priests and ministers stay away from *us*. But Dorothy gives us a pep talk. She says things like How can people be against abortion and birth control, then send boys off to war when they reach eighteen?"

"Not everybody *is* against birth control, though," Tommy said.

"Catholics are. What if war was forbidden to all Catholics?"

"It'd be hard to have a war then," I said.

"It'd be hard to have a war if the government told the truth, too. What if they said, Look, this has to be done. We're going to do it. Some of you will come back blind, some without your legs, or with an arm missing, some deaf, some will come back crazy . . . that is *if* you come back at all."

"I didn't know we were going to have lunch here," Tommy said.

"Did you think I could afford to take you out?" Bud laughed.

"*I* could buy us lunch," I said. "Aunt Lizzie gave me twenty-five dollars for my birthday last month."

"Good!" Tommy started to put his tray back in the stack. "Lunch on Jubal!"

Bud retrieved the tray and handed it to Tommy. "Let's eat here," he said. "I'm on duty."

"I'd love to treat us!" I said. I didn't know how I'd eat in that place without getting sick from the smell. I wished I had some Vicks VapoRub with me. Before I'd become used to mucking out the stables, I'd put a dab in my nostrils to get past the odor.

"Be sure to take a napkin and silver," Bud said. "Jubal, there's cocoa. You don't have to drink coffee."

"I drink coffee now," I said proudly.

Before I knew it, we were carrying trays of bread, chili, cookies, and coffee back to a table in the huge dining room. It was a shabby place with stained walls, the paint peeling, and radiators hissing and clanking. On one wall was a large, gold-framed painting of Jesus with his arms around a white man and a Negro, who were shaking hands.

"Why does everybody keep their coats on?" Tommy asked. "It's not cold in here."

"They don't want them stolen, so watch yours," said Bud. "How's Quinn doing?"

I told him Quinn was his old self. If he was out in the paddock and he saw Daria coming, he'd sometimes stamp his front foot, then run around, dancing sideways.

"From what Tommy's written about Daria, she sounds swell!"

"Mr. Hart's crazy about her," Tommy said. "So's little brother, I think."

"Is that right, Jube?" Bud asked.

I shrugged. "I like her. That's not the question."

"What's the question?" Bud said.

I hadn't told Tommy about Radio Dan's rule against "fraternizing" with a Shoemaker. Tommy believed in telling Bud the truth about everything. I didn't see the point in making him feel worse than he already did about what was happening to us because of him.

"The question is does *she* like *me*?" I said.

"Oh, she likes you, Jubie," Tommy said. "She's at the Harts' the minute she's out of Mrs. Ochevsky's. Every single Saturday, Bud." He gave Bud a wink. "Forget Fast Tom. How about Fast Jubal?"

"She comes because of Quinn," I said, "not me."

Then Bud asked what was going on between Mom and Dad. Tommy filled him in on how cranky and sullen Dad was, and how he spent his time at home down in the basement by himself.

I pushed the chili around on my plate and stole glances at the other tables. I was thinking of how Daria'd told me once that I wasn't very sensitive or worldly. She couldn't believe I didn't like poetry. I wondered what *she'd* think of this place. She'd probably feel more sorry for everybody there than sickened by the sight of them, the way I was.

Where had Bud's great caring for other people come from? Why didn't I seem to have it? I kept thinking about things like that while Bud and Tommy talked. I kept thinking I'd never be as good as Bud, and maybe never be able to tell a draft board I was a CO.

"I wish Dad had come along," Bud said. "It sounds like he could use a vacation."

"And *leave* the *store*?" Tommy chuckled.

"Do you guys give him any help, or do you spend all your time at the Harts'?"

"He's still got the Warner sisters," Tommy said. "He doesn't need much more help."

"What about weekends?"

"What about them?" Tommy said.

"Are some people still refusing to shop there?" Bud asked.

"The war isn't over, Bud," Tommy said.

"But I thought they weren't going to keep punishing *Dad*," said Bud. "They stopped writing on the windows."

"Yeah, the writing stopped. Now it's yellow Ys."

"You didn't write me about that, Tom."

Tommy shrugged. "And half our customers are gone too."

"Half?"

"You say you want to know these things," Tommy said.

"I do. Why didn't you write me about this?"

Tommy said, "I wasn't sure we'd lost them, but I am now. Our regulars just aren't regular anymore. You could say they're 'infrequent' if they show up at all."

"No wonder Dad's changed."

"That's why I've decided not to make it worse,"

Tommy said. "Because of Dad."

"What do you mean?" Bud asked.

"I mean when I register for the draft, I'm going to go 1AO, not 4E, Bud."

That was news to me.

Bud raised an eyebrow, frowned, was quiet for a second.

"You do what you want to, Tommy," he finally said.

"Maybe it's not what I want, but I'll do it for Dad."

Bud said, "Don't hide behind Dad."

"You're right," said Tommy. "Your letters helped me make up my mind too."

"I wanted you to know the score," Bud said. "That's all."

"Thanks."

Silence.

I broke it. "I'll probably be 4E, like you." I just blurted it out without thinking.

Bud must have seen something in my face that said the thought of being a 4E scared me. "You've got time," he said.

Now the din in the dining room was so loud, Bud was practically shouting. "I can't wait until Hope gets here tomorrow. She's worried sick about Abel. They keep him in solitary most of the time. The guards take turns beating him up."

Tommy asked him how Hope knew that.

"There's a Jehovah's Witness in the same prison. He wrote Hope about it."

"Mr. Hart knows about the solitary, but not about the beatings!"

"Abel wouldn't want him to know!"

At the next table a man in a wool jacket and a stocking cap was sitting quietly crying. The men on either side of him went on eating.

"What's the matter with *him?*" Tommy said.

"A lot of people here have a sadness," said Bud.

"Can we get out of here?" I said.

"You didn't eat," Bud answered.

"Yeah, let's get out of here," Tommy said. "Let's take a walk. It stinks in here."

Bud got a coat and walked a few blocks with us. It was raining lightly. The street was jammed with traffic, horns blowing, smoke from truck tailpipes, pushcarts with hot dogs and pretzels.

"That's some coat!" Tommy said to Bud.

It was moth-eaten, with sleeves that ended above Bud's wrists.

"I grabbed it from the clothes bin. If you'd like to look there, you can have anything you find. Everything's free."

"I hope you're not going to wear that coat tonight," Tommy said.

"I'm not like you, Tom. I wait till the last minute to decide what to wear."

Tommy gave him the elbow and Bud laughed. "I have to get back now," he said. He handed Tommy an envelope. "Look this over later and see if you can draw something to go with it."

"What is it?"

"It's going to be a letter to newspaper editors, and we'll make up some posters for reception rooms in hospitals. Make it look good, if you can."

"Okay. We'll see you tonight, Bud. Mike's treat, right?"

"Mike and Lizzie are taking us, yeah."

"I'm surprised *you* got an invitation," said Tommy.

"Lizzie's doing it for Mom, but there won't be a fight."

"If either you or Lizzie, or Mike, open your mouths, there will be," Tommy said.

"No, Mike's taken care of it," said Bud. "We're eating at Asti."

"And you can't fight there?" said Tommy.

"You'll see," Bud said.

★ ★ ★

FOURTEEN

That afternoon Natalia took Tommy and me for a walk around Greenwich Village. When we got to Bedford Street, she said she was going to show us the narrowest house in New York City, built in 1873.

We stopped at 75½, and she said, "A famous poet named Edna St. Vincent Millay lived here."

"'World, I cannot hold thee near enough,'" I said.

Natalia said, "Close, Jubal. It's 'O world, I cannot hold thee close enough.' How come you know that poem?"

"Someone I know knows it."

"Darie Daniel, his girlfriend," Tommy said.

"She doesn't know she's my girlfriend," I said.

"Maybe you ought to tell her."

"You're a fine one to talk, Natalia," I said.

Tommy said, "I remember a Millay poem we studied when I went to Friends school. It was called 'Conscientious Objector.' 'I shall die, but that is all I shall do for Death.'"

"Another line goes, 'I am not on his payroll,'" Natalia said. "She wasn't talking about this war, though."

"How do you know?" Tommy asked.

"Because I know. She hates the Nazis! Have you ever

heard of a village in Czechoslovakia called Lidice?"

Tommy shook his head.

"Of course not! Our schools don't teach one damn thing about what's happening to the Jews!" She sounded like Aunt Lizzie.

"What happened in Lidice?" Tommy asked her.

"The Nazis killed every single man and fifty-two women—the rest were shipped off to concentration camps!"

"I didn't know that," Tommy said.

"How could you? That's why the Writers' War Board asked Edna St. Vincent Millay to write a poem about it. It's called 'The Murder of Lidice.' I know because one of our tenants is on that board. We were invited to a reading of the poem." Natalia never looked at Tommy when she talked to him. Every time Tommy looked at her, she got red. She hadn't lost any weight since Christmas, but she seemed more grown up. She'd stopped saying "Damnation!" and she hadn't yet told me one dirty joke.

When we reached Sheridan Square, she said, "I know something your girlfriend would like, Jubal."

She led us into a drugstore that sold handmade greeting cards. There was one with a picture of the house on Bedford Street.

"Send her this," Natalia said.

I turned it over. It had a quote from one of Millay's poems.

I know I am but summer to your heart,
And not the full four seasons of the year.

You can say that again, I thought. I would have sent it to Daria if it hadn't had that verse on it. But I shelled out two cents for it anyway. It would be a good souvenir of the trip.

When we arrived back at 57 Charles Street, we could hear from the hall a discussion between Lizzie and Mike, not meant for our ears.

"Why did she ever marry him, anyway?" Mike was saying. "She could have done a lot better than that."

"I might have married him myself. You should have seen Efram back in those days!"

"Thanks a lot, sweetheart! What was I? Chopped liver?"

"You were my mental giant, darling. If you marry a mental giant, your marriage has a better chance of lasting than if you marry Handsome Harry."

"Their marriage isn't in trouble because of Efram. It's Bud."

Natalia shouted, "Hello! We're home and we can hear you!"

"I'm not saying anything I wouldn't say to Bud's face," Mike said as we walked into the living room. Shakespeare's blue eyes narrowed, and his black tail flagged. He leaped from Mike's lap and ran off with his ruff up.

"But tonight is not the night to say *anything* to Bud's face! It's my sister's birthday," Lizzie said.

I changed the subject. "We saw the Millay house."

"I bet that gave you a thrill," Mike said. His paintings were all around the room. Lizzie called him a "social realist." He painted coal miners with blackened faces and red eyes, tenement life, factory workers, all grim scenes.

Dad said Mike was a card-carrying Communist, that he could afford to be because he'd come from a rich family. The town house Dad had led me to believe would be filled with loose living was a disappointment that way. It was red brick, well kept, its brass railing and doorknobs gleaming. Whoever else was in residence there didn't show themselves or make noise.

Before we went out that night, Tommy showed me what Bud wanted him to illustrate.

THE POWER OF WORDS
Mental illness seems to be a disgrace when we describe it with the old ignorant words. Why not use "patient" instead of "inmate"? How about "mental hospital" instead of "insane asylum"? Over 600,000 Americans are now hospitalized because of mental illness. Most of them are receiving pitifully inadequate treatment and care. We can start to change things by changing our vocabulary when we speak of them.

"What can you draw to go with that?" I asked Tommy.

"Maybe a bird flying."

"Or a flock of them."

"Something changing," Tommy said. "What's changing?"

"Draw Dad."

"Jubal, the Comedian," Tommy said.

★ ★ ★

Là ci darem la mano,
Là mi dirai di sì.

"We're going to hear a lot of longhair music," Bud leaned down to say to me, "so prepare yourself."

"I like *this* opera," I said. "It's Mozart's *Don Giovanni.*"

"Good for you, little brother."

I could almost hear Daria's voice singing out: *Calma, calma il tuo tormento.*

Asti was in the Village, on East 12th Street. We'd walked to it from Mike and Lizzie's, on Charles Street. Daria would have thought she'd died and gone to heaven there. It was filled with the sounds of opera. While you ate dinner, everyone sang around you: waiters serving you, bartenders, other customers; even Mike let go during *Aïda.*

The first thing I noticed was that there weren't a lot of servicemen there. I could see only two sailors at one big table, and an Army lieutenant at another. I was glad of that. I wondered if Bud ever paid attention to things like that when he was away from the hospital, if he was ever uncomfortable in places where there were a lot of men in uniform.

He hadn't worn the old coat he'd had on that afternoon. He wore a tweed jacket with a flannel shirt and knit tie. He had a fresh haircut and shave he said he got free at a barbers' school on the Bowery. I heard Mike mutter, "Trust *you* to take a free ride," but Bud didn't hear him.

Lizzie looked more glamorous than ever with her blond hair wrapped behind her head, a black dress cut low, a string of pearls around her neck. And Lizzie had talked my mother into accepting one of her suits, a black silk that looked great with this white silk blouse that Lizzie said was a present from Einstein, Marx, and Shakespeare. I was glad Dad wasn't there to throw his hands up at that idea.

Bud had been right: Mike had the right restaurant. Although Natalia had glommed onto Tommy on the walk there, and then sat beside him at the big round table we occupied, Tommy didn't have to talk much. Everyone was singing. Bud was forking down spaghetti like someone straight off a desert island, grabbing the Chianti bottle by the neck now and again to offer some to everyone, drinking faster than any of the others. I'd never seen Bud drink anything but an occasional beer. And neither Bud nor Tommy smoked in front of Mom.

Both Mike and Lizzie were trying not to react to Bud. The few digs at Bud that Mike made weren't loud enough for Bud to hear. And Mike liked to sing, too.

After a few hours waiters carried in a huge cake singing "Happy Birthday, Dear Winnie," and champagne corks popped.

Mike tried to get Mom to have a glass of champagne, but she wanted "just ginger ale, thank you." Lizzie reminded her how Dad always said when in Rome do as the Romans do. Mom might just as well have been in Rome for all the familiarity she had with a New York City restaurant. She looked smaller, somehow, and a little lost. Lizzie's toast to Mom was too long and too mushy.

I was allowed one glass of champagne, which I gulped down. I wanted Natalia to stand back-to-back with me, to see if I wasn't finally as tall as she was, or taller.

"Not now." Bud stopped me from getting up with his hand on my wrist.

"Bud, how's Hope?" Lizzie asked.

"She's okay. You'll see. She works too hard, and there aren't enough recipes that use beans. That's what she's got the most of down there. They have beans for every meal."

I was expecting some sarcasm from Mike about hungry G.I.'s somewhere who'd give their eyeteeth for beans, but he was busy singing something from *Carmen* along with the others.

When Tommy went to the men's, I followed him in and said, "I *know* I'm taller than Natalia now. I'm as tall as Daria, too!"

"I know you've got a buzz on," Tommy said.

"Me? On one glass of champagne."

"Yeah, you, little brother."

"I'd like it if you and Bud wouldn't call me that anymore."

"Okay."

"Are you making the announcement tonight about going 1AO?"

"No, and don't you."

"Why? Uncle Mike and Aunt Lizzie will be glad to hear it."

"That's why. I don't care what they'd be glad to hear. I'm not going to put Bud in a bad light, as though I made a great decision and he didn't."

I said, "But you believe he really *didn't*, don't you, Tommy?"

"You're tight, Jubal. Let's talk about it tomorrow."

"Tight." I scoffed at the idea. "On one teensy tiny glass of the bubbly?" We walked out.

There was a woman photographer going from table to table, wanting to sell pictures she'd take of guests.

"Over here!" Mike shouted at her. He behaved like a big shot, tipping her five dollars, ordering copies for everyone at the table.

I was missing Daria. I couldn't wait to ask her if she knew that Edna St. Vincent Millay had written a poem called "Conscientious Objector." If she didn't, I doubted that I'd tell her it wasn't about *this* war.

I wished she could just meet Bud. Maybe she'd be able to understand why he chose to be a CO. He looked so happy that night, grinning, his blue eyes flashing. I think he was glad to be with family, despite all our differences: We *were* family, and we were together having a good time.

Bud nudged me and said, "If you're not going to eat the rest of your cake, I'll eat it."

"Okay. Pour me a little champagne, please."

"Don't get me in trouble, little brother. You've had enough."

"What I've had enough of is being called little brother."

Bud laughed as he reached for my plate. "Good boy! Speak up for yourself, Jubal! Always! I thought it was an affectionate moniker. I didn't know you didn't like it." He slung his arm around my shoulder. "Jubal, I won't call you that ever again."

"Hear that, Mom?" I said. "Bud's never going to call me little brother ever again."

There was a hush in the restaurant as a woman in a red gown stood and sang. Bud said her name, and said she was a famous opera star.

She was singing *"Un Bel Di"* from *Madama Butterfly*. Daria sometimes sang it. She said she was singing "someday he'll come."

I decided to whisper what I'd tried to tell Mom. "Hey, Mom, Bud's never going to call me little—" Then I looked at her, and I couldn't finish the sentence.

Mom was sitting there with tears streaming down

her face, like the man I'd seen at the soup kitchen that afternoon.

I remembered Bud saying some people had a sadness, and I wondered if Mom's was about Dad.

FIFTEEN

I tried to explain to Daria what a Broadway musical was like, but there was no way I could do the experience justice. Even Hope jumped to her feet with most everyone in the audience, to applaud at the end of *Oklahoma!*

It was Aunt Lizzie's treat. She'd purposely picked out something that didn't have anything in it about the war, or the Jews, or *anything* remotely controversial. Hope had come up from Virginia. She and Bud stayed down at the Dorothy Day shelter.

"In the same room?" Daria asked.

"Probably. They're practically married."

"But they're *not.*"

"No, they're not."

"Why not?" Daria said.

I told her what Bud had told Tommy and me: that there was no way to know how long the war would last, and that if Hope ever wanted to get another job, it would make it harder for her if she was married to a CO. And even if they ignored that and got married anyway, it wouldn't be easy to find a place to live together. Nearly all tourist homes near CPS camps didn't welcome guests who had anything to do with the camps. Some even put up signs saying so. It was the same with landlords who had apartments or rooms to rent, not that Bud and Hope could afford either thing.

"Why didn't you send me a card?" Daria teased. If she hadn't said that, I might never have told her I had one for her, with me.

I pulled it out of the inside pocket of my jacket and handed it to her.

She studied it awhile, then grinned and said, "Oh, Jubal! Did you go to Edna St. Vincent Millay's house?"

"Sure. My cousin took us," I said. "Did you know Millay wrote a poem called 'Conscientious Objector'? It's against war."

"That's not about this war!" Daria said the same thing Natalia had said. "This war is different!" She took the card from me and said, "I'll put this in my Bible. I'll always save it. Those lines are from one of my favorite Millay sonnets! I'll bet you didn't send it because those two lines were on it, and they were too sentimental."

She'd made my ears red. I could feel how hot they were. I mumbled something about not wanting to spend the penny for postage.

We were on the one-thirty bus to Doylestown. Daria was wearing a green sweater that matched her eyes. I loved her hands with the long fingers she kept manicured but didn't color. The only makeup I didn't like girls wearing was nail polish. Mom never wore makeup or jewelry and used to shake her head at anyone who did. She'd softened some the past few years. She wasn't as strict. Last Christmas I'd heard her tell

Lizzie she could get used to Lizzie wearing the bright-red lipstick, but not the mascara and eyeliner, and *not* the nail polish.

Daria opened her pocketbook and took out a letter.

"Since you thought of me while you were in New York, I'll show you something that made me think of you."

It was V-mail, with an APO return address and the name Sgt. Daniel Daniel Jr.

She said, "Before you read it, I want you to know my father thinks it's because of battle fatigue, and I think so, too."

"Okay . . . can I read it now?"

She nodded.

It was written on onion-skin airmail paper.

I wish now that I hadn't nagged at Dean to join up. My best buddy was killed yesterday, lying off the path on his back, arms outstretched, this look of horror frozen in his eyes. We're all getting killed before we've even lived as adults, and what for? Just to kill Japs. Make fodder of them or end up fodder. Here's a poem going around:

To kill is our business, and that's what we do.
It's the main job of war for me and for you.
And the more Japs we rub out,
    the sooner we're through.

How naive I was to think this had any glory in it! The more I kill, the farther away Sweet Creek gets. There isn't anything I can recommend about war. At times I think I'm going to die here in this damn jungle.

I handed it back to her.

"Do you think it sounds like battle fatigue?" she asked me.

"I think it sounds like the truth," I said.

"You *would* say that. . . . It's strange, because Dean complained about the saltwater showers he took aboard ship and then about the wormy rice and Spam wherever he is now, but it's ordinary griping, you know? He loves being a Marine!"

"He hasn't been one as long as Danny has."

"That's what Daddy said. Danny has battle fatigue."

"Why couldn't it just be that he hates it, that's it's horrible?"

"Jubal, you know Danny. He wouldn't complain like that if there wasn't something wrong. He's a real Marine!"

"The something that's wrong is the *killing*, Daria. He makes that clear enough."

"I knew I shouldn't show it to you."

"I'm not going to say any more about it. Okay?"

"Don't tell *anyone* either. Please?"

"I won't."

"My father didn't even want it to leave our house!"

She put the postcard and the V-mail back into her pocketbook.

"Thanks for showing it to me," I said.

"Do you know why I did?" She didn't wait for my answer. "I showed it to you because the one thing I don't like about you is the way you defend Bud."

I looked at her, amazed. "Did you think that letter would change my mind?"

"I think it's not fair for Danny to have to go through that when certain others get out of it . . . when certain others won't even volunteer to be medics!"

"We've talked about this before. I'm not going to argue with you."

I could have. Something had been happening to me since I'd been to New York. Maybe seeing how Bud chose to live his life made me want mine to count for something. I'd also been reading back copies of *The Catholic Worker*, a pacifist newspaper published by Dorothy Day, and some pamphlets Bud had given me. I knew for sure now that when it came my turn, I wanted to witness. Bud had said not to choose 4E just because he had. Either I wouldn't stick with it, or else I'd be miserable. But I'd begun to believe it was the only way I *could* register for the draft and have any respect for myself. The more I prayed about it, the surer I was.

On the train ride home from New York I kept thinking how excited Bud was about his work at Shenandoah. It didn't even seem to bother him that although he received a salary as a hospital attendant, it was automatically forwarded to the federal government. He didn't see a nickel of it. *That* would bother *me*. But Bud was full of praise for the new superintendent. There were plans afoot for a front-yard sign that said "Hospital," not "Asylum." This new man wanted all the attendants to call patients Mr. or Mrs. or Miss as a start to restoring their dignity. No more meals on the floor with drinks from the hose.

After Daria's voice lesson I rode Baby Boy and she rode Quinn. We went up into the Chester Hills. It was a warm May afternoon with the sun shining down on us.

When we reached Chester Park, the highest point, we got off our horses to take in the view.

"I don't mean to be hard on you, Jubal," she said. "I shouldn't hold you responsible for what Bud does."

"It's all right," I said. "I'm proud of what he's doing."

She let that go by. "I never had a knack for making friends. I was always with Danny or Dean. By the time they went off to war, it was too late." She turned and smiled. "You're my best friend."

"I guess you're *my* best friend, too."

"You *guess*? Do you have a lot of friends at school?"

"I think of you sometimes as more than a friend."

Hot face again; I wished I could quit that!

Daria didn't say anything, so I said, "Don't worry, I'm not planning to spoil things with a big pronouncement of any kind."

She gave me one of her slanted smiles. "If you want to kiss me, come to the Catholic Armed Forces Day next Saturday. I'm in the Kissing Booth. Ten cents a kiss, Jubal."

"No thanks."

"Because the money goes to the war?"

"Not only that. When I kiss someone, I want her to want it as much as I do."

She smiled up at me. "'Come slowly—Eden!'"

"What does that mean?"

"'Come slowly—Eden! . . . As the fainting bee— Reaching late his flower, Round her chamber hums.' It was written by this old maid who wrote poetry I could swoon over. She was a recluse who never left her family home in Amherst, Massachusetts. I guess she took life *too* slowly."

"What poet is that?"

"Emily Dickinson," said Daria.

"I don't read a lot of poetry," I said.

"You don't read *any*." She gave my sleeve a tug. "You should, too. Don't you want to be civilized?"

"Who do I start with? Are there any good male poets?"

She hit her forehead with her palm and groaned. She said, "Did you ever hear of William Shakespeare?"

"To be or not to be," I said. "That is the *quest tee own*."

She continued, "William Butler Yeats? William Wordsworth? Robert Browning, John Greenleaf —"

"I know! I know! I was just kidding!"

"You weren't kidding." She walked back to Quinn chuckling and muttering to herself, *Are there any good male poets!*

We headed back down the hill. In the shallows, where the cattails grew, a red-winged blackbird flashed by. We came to the stretch of newly plowed, rich, red-brown fields that ran for miles before we'd reach the paddock. She let Quinn go. I saw her long brown hair blowing in the wind. I couldn't catch them. That seemed to be the problem: I couldn't catch her.

★ ★ ★

SIXTEEN

That summer Daria worked on the New Jersey shore as a junior counselor at a camp for kids with polio. It was a summer that seemed never to end. I was working alongside Luke Casper, whose wife had written a Dear John one day and run off with a sailor. He would try to joke about it, say he didn't mind the fact she'd dumped him, but she'd taken the sugar ration book with her. He kept telling me that Daria looked like her, that I shouldn't let Daria get away. It did no good to tell him I'd never had a claim on her in the first place.

I sent Daria a long letter all about the horses and certain songs I liked: "You'll Never Know," and "Taking a Chance on Love." I asked her what she was listening to that she liked. I told her it was lonely without her.

I got a postcard back saying she was having the best summer of her life. As for songs, she liked "Brazil," and "Pistol Packin' Mama." From then on I wrote only postcards, six, and she sent me two more.

I listened every night, at eleven, to WBEA's rebroadcast of Radio Dan. I knew he talked about his family from time to time, and I didn't want to miss anything he might say about Daria. He called her Darie. There were several versions of his theme song, "Slap Your Sides," at the end. She sang them all. One night he had this very confiding tone, as though he was telling you something he'd been mulling over. "You know," he crooned, "I can't help hoping that one of our servicemen, one who's fought the good fight and is ready now to come home and settle down . . . well, I hope this fellow will connect with my Darie someday. I can tell you right now I don't want a son-in-law who hasn't been part of this . . . and I don't mean sitting at a desk, or driving an ambulance over a battlefield *after* the battle's over. . . . Call me narrow-minded, but I tell Darie these drugstore cowboys who aren't in the service, for whatever excuse, aren't fit to ring our front doorbell. You think you're going to take *my* little girl out? In a pig's eye, buster!"

It was the summer Sicily was invaded and Rome was bombed. Lizzie would call Mom, and after they'd talked awhile, she'd ask for Tommy and me. She'd say things like "The entire Warsaw ghetto is rubble now. Fifteen thousand Jews died, and another fifty thousand were shipped off to death camps." . . . She'd say, "Can you hear me, boys? Do you realize what's going on in Europe?"

Tommy had broken up with Lillie Light because he wanted to join the Army. She and her whole family were the sort of strict Mennonites who maybe didn't travel by wagon but did paint the chrome on their cars black so they didn't look flashy. They were sternly opposed to the war, even to someone serving as a noncombatant.

Tommy registered for the draft, but when he took

his physical, he was classified 4F because of a perforated eardrum.

He couldn't believe it. He said lucky thing the war was probably going to be over before I had to make my decision, because one of us should serve.

"I *won't*," I said. That was the first time I'd really made it clear, and I was a little surprised when the words came out of my mouth. But I was proud of myself, too.

"You won't have to worry about it anyway, Jube."

"Bud says it could go on for years."

"How would Bud know?" Tommy said. "And Aunt Lizzie's right about the Jews, too! Hitler's killing all the Jews! If Hitler has his way, no one's going to be safe."

"And when Hitler's defeated, there'll be other dictators to come along," I said. "There'll be other races to destroy. The only way to stop war is for ordinary citizens to start saying No! I'm not going!"

"I know all the pacifist arguments, Jube. I went to SCFS, too, remember. But this war *is* different!"

Even though the Warner sisters were over sixty, they left Shoemaker's for higher-paying jobs at Wride Foods. So after school Tommy worked for Dad, and Mom went in too, sometimes.

Wrides was Sweet Creek's only "essential industry." A lot of females got jobs there. Tommy was dating one named Rose Garten. She had graduated from Sweet Creek High the year before and was one year older than Tommy. Her family were Catholics who lived in

Blooming Glen. Tommy complained that she smelled of onions, but her graph had gone from 50 to 80 in a few weeks.

The last Saturday in August Tommy let Dad run the store by himself, so he could transport Baby Boy and Heavenly. They'd been sold to Orland Gish, a rich Mennonite with a farm in Lancaster.

A week later Luke Casper found a new horse who came with the name "Ike" after General Eisenhower. Mr. Hart wasn't a fan of the military, so he renamed him Tyke, because he was smaller than most horses. The horse was restless, too; he didn't like to mind.

He acted so wild, I had to keep him out in the paddock.

That was when Daria came back. After her music lesson, just as I'd finished mucking out the stalls, she came by the Harts' and we went for a ride. I was on Tyke, who was trying to go where he wanted to go, not where we wanted to.

All the things I'd stored up to say to Daria, about my feelings for her, went unsaid. She was suddenly beautiful, tan, and happy-looking. Whatever made me think she'd give a damn what *I* thought of her? She kept talking about what a glorious summer she'd had: that helping people was what she planned to do with her life.

"Maybe you should be a nurse," I said.

She pushed back her long hair and eyed me. "I'd rather be a doctor."

"What kind?"

"Maybe a psychiatrist," she said.

I told her about Abel Hart being sent to a psychiatric prison up north, after he was beaten up again. Mr. Hart went to see him and he said he hardly recognized Abel, and Abel didn't know who he was. He had bruises on his face and arms from the beatings he'd received. His red hair had turned white, and his teeth chattered when he spoke, as though he was freezing. He'd told Mr. Hart he didn't have to sleep anymore. He said he'd found the secret of eternal life.

"The Army ought to discharge him," Daria said.

"He's not in the Army, remember?"

"I keep forgetting." She was riding Quinn, who was delighted she'd come back and was stepping high because of it.

"Daddy told me Tommy actually registered for the draft," she said.

When Tommy told Mom and Dad the Army wouldn't take him, Dad had looked at Mom and said, "I bet thee are glad, Mother, hah?" It was meant as sarcasm. He'd begun speaking the plain language to her in this snide way, accompanied by a tiny, mean smile.

Dad had stopped going to Rotary Tuesdays because there was always a hometown boy on leave or furlough, telling about his experiences in the war. Then there were the fellow Rotarians, who snubbed Dad or asked snide questions about Bud. *Don't tell me your boy still won't fight?*

"Daddy said it took guts for Tommy to try and join

the Army," Daria continued, "considering the example Bud set."

"It takes guts to be 4E too."

"I knew you'd say that," said Daria.

"Then why bring it up?"

"I keep hoping you'll change your mind."

In Bud's last letter he had written that a few more of the COs were changing their minds. They were giving in to pressure from their families, from the war news, and from their consciences, and they were asking for re-classification. They were being reassigned as 1AO, same as Tommy'd hoped to be: noncombatant service-men.

I told Daria a little about Bud's work at the hospital, that he wrote describing the scorn institutions had for patients who were feeble, incontinent, angry, and most often all three.

> Just getting them cleaned, dressed, and ready for breakfast takes until lunch. I come on duty at 7 A.M. and start by putting tooth-paste on 50 toothbrushes. Before we rigged up showers here, they would bathe all in the same tub, one by one, not bothering to change the water. There is a big American Indian called Sky Hawk. You should see the size of him! He doesn't speak but sometimes will howl like a dog, his fists up, ready to punch you. The way they used to discipline

him was to tether him to his iron bed minus the mattress, facedown naked, lower a Turkish towel in a bucket of water, then swat him with it. Leave him there all day, crying and soiling himself. All because he did something like steal a piece of toast from someone's breakfast plate.

"I want to help people, but I wouldn't want that job," Daria said. "It's thankless, isn't it?"

"Bud says those patients haven't been given the chance to see what they can do. Places like that just give them custodial care."

"If *that*, it sounds like.... Oh, there are things I admire about Bud. But I agree with something Daddy said."

"What?"

"That Bud is putting out the fire in the house across the street when his own house is on fire."

I didn't bother to try and answer that, but I wondered if people in Sweet Creek knew about Mom and Dad. At home Dad was either making snide remarks or acting like Mom wasn't there. Was he doing it in the store, too?

Last August, when my buddy Marty Allen and I had joined the volunteers painting the trim on SCFS, there had been a new sign behind glass at the front entrance.

I WILL LAY DOWN MY LIFE IF NEED BE, BUT I WILL NOT TAKE SOMEONE ELSE'S.

Kids had written in black crayon on the wall next to it: **WHAT ABOUT HITLER'S? MUSSOLINI'S? TOJO'S?**

Daria and I rode along awhile. The land needed rain badly. Even the trees were dusty.

I announced I'd been reading some poetry.

"Really? I'm impressed!"

"And I like it."

"Who're you reading?"

"His name is Walter Benton!"

"Oh *no*."

"What's the matter?"

"You've been reading *This Is My Beloved*?"

"Yeah. I'm halfway through it."

"That's tacky, Jubal."

"It's not tacky." It was a Natalia Granger recommendation: "Sexy as all get-out!" she'd written across a postcard. She was right.

"Why don't you read serious poets?" Daria asked me.

"Because I don't know what they're talking about."

"But you know what Walter Benton is talking about!" she said.

"I wish I knew *more*."

She laughed over her shoulder at me, then told Quinn to giddyap.

I had some trouble heading Tyke in the direction of the stable, and when we got there finally, Quinn was out in the paddock. Daria was waiting for Tyke and me.

"Now let's pay some attention to this little fellow,"

she said as I got off him. "I bet he belonged to some-one. He looks like the kind of horse people get for their kids. Like a Morgan."

Together we brushed and curried Tyke. We sham-pooed him and scrubbed his legs so his stockings turned golden, then shampooed his tail until it was blue-black.

All the while, Daria crooned to him. "I know what you want, Tyke. . . . I'm going to take good care of you, Tyke. . . . Do you hear me?" . . . I shut my eyes and thought of her saying some of that stuff to me. After, when we turned him out, he pranced and snorted. He sauntered by Quinn as though he were tipping his hat to him.

We were about to leave when Luke Casper ambled down from the office. Sometimes the way he looked at Daria from head to toe made me want to punch him. He told Daria she was going to "catch it" when she got home.

"What am I going to catch, Luke?" Daria laughed. "Am I going to catch the chicken pox?"

"Radio Dan's having a fit!"

"Why? He knows I take the horses out."

"I'll bet he doesn't know you take them out with Jubal."

"Did you tell him?"

"No."

"You're a sweetheart, Luke!" Daria said.

"Yeah, thanks, Luke," I said.

"I was doing *her* a favor. I wasn't doing you one, Jubal." We'd never been buddies. Religion was foreign to him, particularly one like Friends. He didn't dare make cracks around Mr. Hart, but he'd bait me sometimes about the war. He'd say, "Did you see in the newspapers that your pal Adolf bombed London again?"

He was 4F because of a hernia.

There were times, too, when he'd try to get me to drink whiskey with him. Then he'd say, "Okay, don't drink anything. Just hang out while *I* drink." I knew he was really lonely.

"Your daddy's called here twice," he told Daria. "He's probably got fire coming out of his nose by now!"

"I *bet* he has," Daria said to me as we walked away from Casper. "It's almost *five*, Jubal. How could I forget the time this way?"

"Don't call Luke 'sweetheart,'" I said. "He'll take it the wrong way."

"Oh, he's harmless. I think he looks like Jimmy Cagney. Did you see him in *Yankee Doodle Dandy*? I love that movie!"

"I saw him in *The Roaring Twenties* with Humphrey Bogart. . . . But don't kid with Luke," I said. "You'll give him ideas. He says you look like his ex."

"I *wish*. She was gorgeous! I like it that you're protective, Jubal."

We headed toward the bus stop, through fields filled with Queen Anne's lace and ironweed. Barn swallows were swooping in the air, and the haze from the heat was blurring the sight of the Welsh Mountains.

She was walking ahead of me when she said, "My

times with you are the best times, Jubal."

"Me, too."

"We're lucky, Jubal . . . lucky lucky lucky."

When I got home, Mom was mixing the white margarine with the yellow food coloring, to make it look like butter.

"Why don't you just leave it white?" I asked her.

"Your father won't eat it white."

"Caesar rules," I said.

"What did you say?" Mom looked over at me with this tired expression in her eyes, as though she was just about at the end of her rope.

"I didn't say anything. Forget it."

"I heard you, Jubal. . . . I don't like you showing your father disrespect!"

"What about the way *he* acts? Sitting downstairs brooding, and when he does come up, he's got nothing nice to say to us! He mocks you by speaking the plain language to you! He just orders Tommy and me and you around: Do this, do that, no please or thank you!"

"He needs help. Particularly with heavy work. You know how hard it is for Daddy to ask for help."

"Since when can't he do heavy work? He's getting a paunch, you know. Maybe he needs more exercise."

"No," Mom said sharply. "That's not what he needs. He needs to rest."

"From what? From his duties as air-raid warden? That's about all the exercise he gets. How long since he's been to meeting?"

He hadn't been there in months. Tommy and Mom and I rarely missed a Sunday. He stayed down in his cellar retreat, where the only one who ever went to see what he was doing was Mahatma.

Mom rinsed her hands. She turned around and faced me with an angry look. It matched the spirit of the sudden clap of thunder not too far away. "Daddy's not well, Jubal! He's got problems in his body as well as his spirit. Doctor Sincerbeaux called me and told me Daddy's heart misses beats."

"I'm sorry, Mom."

"I know you're making good money at the Harts', and I know you're sending some to Bud," Mom said. "That's fine. I'm proud of you. But you have to help *here*. Before you volunteer to paint that school, you should find out what needs to be done *here*!"

A jagged edge of lightning lit up the sky outside. It was the answer to our prayers: a heavy rain starting down.

I said, "Mom, make a list. Put everything that needs doing on it."

"Thanks, Jubal. . . . Tommy will help too, although he goes to the store right after school every day."

"I don't need Tommy's help," I said. "He does enough as it is."

She said, "Be patient with Daddy. Today of all days, try to understand what it's been like for him."

"What happened today?"

"You've been at the Harts'. The neighbors have been up and down the block telling everyone."

"Telling everyone what, Mom?"

That was when I found out why Radio Dan had been trying to get in touch with Daria. It was the first I heard that Dean Daniel had been killed in the central Pacific, on one of the Gilbert Islands.

I remembered when Dean was a junior counselor at Camp Quannacut, how he'd screamed when he saw a daddy longlegs in his sneaker. . . . And I remembered seeing him hoist his seabag onto his shoulder, and wave good-bye in the Trenton train station, the same night Bud left for his CPS camp.

SEVENTEEN

The next afternoon, a Sunday, I carried a macaroni-and-cheese casserole down the street to the Daniels.

It was received through a crack in the door by Daria's mother, with no invitation to come inside.

"Here's Jubal now!" my mother said into the telephone as I got back home. "Jubal? It's Darie Daniel."

"I'm sorry about Dean," I said.

"Thank you very much," she said, and I knew from her tone of voice she wasn't alone. "But I wish you would come now and take back this casserole. We aren't comfortable accepting it, Jubal. We don't want anything from Bud Shoemaker's house, particularly now."

Mom could hear me, so I just said, "Whatever you say."

"The casserole will be on our front porch for you to pick up immediately."

There was a click.

"She's such a nice girl," my mother said. "What did she want?"

"We were going horseback riding later," I lied. "Naturally she can't keep the date."

I used walking Mahatma as an excuse to retrieve the dish. There was a row of hedges a few doors down, and

I emptied the contents into the branches for the birds.

Back at our house Mom was reading the Bible in the living room. Dad was at the dining-room table, drinking coffee and looking over the Sunday newspapers.

I washed the casserole dish and hid it under some mixing bowls.

Then I went back and sat by Dad.

"Did you see the latest from Orland Gish?" he asked me.

Orland Gish sometimes took out ads in the Philadelphia newspapers. They'd be full page, and they'd quote pacifists like A. A. Milne, author of the Pooh series for children; Albert Schweitzer; Gandhi; and Henry David Thoreau. Sometimes I'd think thank God for him, because he was a prosperous Mennonite farmer with a lot of land, the kind of man people respected and admired. Not a coconut.

Dad passed me a full page toward the back of *The Philadelphia Compass*.

* * *

WAR BULLETINS

· Probably the heaviest casualties since the war began have been on the Russian front, where in the first year of the war 3,500,000 Germans were killed.

· Soviet losses in the first year of the war were estimated between 8,000,000 and 10,000,000 dead; 3,000,000 missing, wounded, or held prisoner.

- Deputy Prime Minister Clement Attlee told the House of Commons (June 1942) that the total military casualties of the British Empire for the past two years of the war were 48,973 killed; 46,363 wounded; and 8,458 held prisoner.

- 25,000 defenders of Bataan killed by Japanese on 65-mile march to prisoners-of-war camp, another 22,000 died in first two months there.

- 5,188 Japanese killed (by actual count) in the Tulagi-Guadalcanal campaign.

DYING TO HEAR MORE?

Or would you rather hear a saner view of war from Dr. Henry Emerson Fosdick?

"The first person to vote for a declaration of war should be the first soldiers on the battlefield. It is disturbing to the rational mind when the people who dispatch others to the front stand above the fray."

PRAY FOR PEACE

★ ★ ★

Dad stayed in the dining room most of the afternoon, rooting for the St. Louis Cardinals with Tommy. They listened to the game on the radio Tommy and I shared.

I sneaked out and cleaned the garage, #1 on Mom's

task list. I kept thinking about Daria, remembering what she'd said yesterday when we were leaving the Harts'. *We're lucky, Jubal . . . lucky, lucky, lucky.*

All I could do now was wait, see if she'd come to the farm next Saturday. See if she'd call in the meantime.

I worked until sundown. When I went back inside, the game was over but Dad was still sitting at the dining-room table, drinking a hot chocolate that Tommy had made for him. Mom was in the living room knitting in that fast, nervous way of hers when something was upsetting her.

Mr. Hart had just phoned to tell the family that Abel had escaped from prison. There was an all-points bulletin out for him.

"We were waiting for you before we called Bud." Tommy handed me a cup of cocoa.

"I suppose Abel will show up at the farm," I said.

Dad said, "That will be the last place he'll go if there's anything left of his mind."

"They think he went south," Tommy said. "Back to Florida, maybe."

True, I had never taken to Abel. But I hoped he wouldn't be caught by any southern police. I had an idea they'd go harder on him. Even though every southern writer seemed to be fond of crazies (at Friends School we were just reading Carson McCullers' *The Heart Is a Lonely Hunter*), they were *their* crazies, not crazies from up north who didn't want to fight in the war.

★ ★ ★

EIGHTEEN

That Christmas was the first year Natalia didn't come to Pennsylvania with Aunt Lizzie. Natalia had been on a rigid diet, Lizzie told us, but she wanted to keep the reason secret until she could tell us herself.

I figured she'd finally found a boyfriend; should I try and get Tommy's favorite socks back?

Natalia had sent Tommy a tie from Brooks Brothers in New York, and I got two books. One was an old novel by F. Scott Fitzgerald, *Tender Is the Night*, with a paper clip marking one page. The other was *A Tree Grows in Brooklyn*, sans paper clip.

Lizzie had given me two books, too, both by Ernie Pyle, the Pulitzer Prize war reporter.

Sunday morning we all went off to Friends, except for my father.

I stood outside the meetinghouse for a while with Tommy. He smoked a Camel with the long cigarette holder Lizzie had bought him for Christmas. She'd found it at Dunhill. She said it was identical to the one President Roosevelt had.

I was hoping for a glimpse of Daria. She'd be attending St. Peter's across the street. Already the organ music was thundering through the stained-glass windows, and families were hurrying inside. They always began promptly at nine, while we started gathering in a random way until the room seemed full, and even then sometimes no one spoke for ten or twenty more minutes.

"Shall I light another Camel?" Tommy asked me. "Or do you think maybe Darie's already inside?"

She hadn't been to the Harts' since Dean's death. The only times I saw her were evenings when I'd walk Mahatma down the street. Sometimes she'd be standing by the piano, singing, while her mother played. Sometimes she'd be sitting at the desk in the living room. I'd see the back of her long brown hair. Instead of two blue stars in the window, one was gold now, since Dean had been killed.

Radio Dan hadn't done what I thought he would. He hadn't poured it on, or tried to milk the situation. In a quieter, more solemn tone than usual, he talked about Dean. His love of music. His stamp collection. He mentioned that he'd been an Eagle Scout and a Sea Scout.

"Now among the honors he received, among the awards, there will be a Medal of Honor. God bless my boy, and God bless you for your cards and letters."

Right after word of Dean's death, I'd spent almost an hour at Sweet Creek Cards and Stationery trying to find the right sympathy card. One was more awful than the other, but the worst showed a figure disappearing into some clouds, with the line under it advising, "He is not dead—he is just away. . . . " He's *both*, I thought.

I finally bought a card with nothing more on the front than a gold cross. Inside it, I wrote:

> *I'm sorry about Dean, Daria. Please call.*
> *Love from Jubal*

I'd gone into the diner a few times, and I'd even dropped in on The Teen Canteen, in the basement of St. Peter's, because a friend from school saw her there one night. There was never any sign of her. Tommy said she was at Sweet Creek High every day, but she disappeared when she saw him coming. She had won a school essay contest about the medal awarded Dean posthumously. An officer in a Marine dress uniform had come to the Daniels' with it, and at St. Peter's there'd been a short memorial service during which Mrs. Daniel had been presented with a folded flag.

For Christmas I'd bought Daria a five-dollar bottle of Evening in Paris perfume. Tommy handed it to her just before school went on vacation. He told her it was from me. He said she'd looked flustered, thanked him, then run off in the other direction.

I knew that at meeting Lizzie was going to get after the Quakers, and I looked down at my shoes while she did. She quoted A. A. Milne, who had done an about-face and come out with a book called *War with Honour*. Bud said Milne had stunned COs everywhere and put a deep wound in pacifist morale.

Lizzie had a long red feather on her hat pointed down toward her chin.

"'One man's fanaticism has cancelled rational argument,'" she began, and several Friends glared up at her. She sank one hand into the pocket of her jacket, the new kind called an Eisenhower.

She continued reading. "'This is a war for the destruction of all Christian and civilised values. Not a war between nations, but a war between Good and Evil. Hitler is the self-elected, self-confessed anti-Christ! Evil is his God.'"

While there was strong pacifist sentiment among all Sweet Creek Quakers, Bud was the only one who'd chosen the 4E classification over the 1AO. Some of the congregation's eligible fathers and sons were already in the service, nearly all as noncombatants.

Still, no one spoke up. Lizzie had the floor and the last word.

If the Sweet Creek Friends were probably resigned to the annual tongue-lashing from Lizzie, Dad was not. Just when he seemed to be calmer—we hadn't had any yellow Ys on our store windows for months— Lizzie'd arrived, dukes up, as usual.

Dad sliced the ham with a hard frown as Lizzie attacked him for not knowing a certain popular song had been composed by a Jew.

"Not that you would know anything Jews do, or have

done to them" was the next thing to come out of her mouth. I think she was a little tight from the Mumm's champagne she'd opened for herself before we'd sat down. She was smiling, but her words were harsh. "If you cared at all, why would you be serving ham to me?"

"Why wouldn't I be serving it to thee?" Dad's voice was mocking.

Mom said, "Lizzie, Tommy chose the menu. You know he always cooks for First Day."

"Lizzie," Tommy said, "I didn't think you or Mike observed dietary laws of any kind."

"Sweetie pie, we don't. Forget it." She raised her glass. She was the only one drinking. She said, "Forget it, forget them, already forgotten in Hitler's concentration camps, soon to go up in smoke—pffft!" A big swallow of champagne.

Tommy said, "Hey, Lizzie, it's Christmastime!"

"Oh, let her continue to run off at the mouth," said Dad. "She's been living too long with those who don't celebrate Christmas."

"What do you mean by that, Efram?" Lizzie's eyes were afire.

"I have never heard that people of the Jewish persuasion celebrate Christmas."

"Dad!" Tommy cried.

"I don't celebrate Christmas either, Efram," Mom said.

I said, "He didn't mean that the way it sounded."

"I'm not eating at the table with you, Efram

Shoemaker!" Lizzie got up and flounced into the living room. Next, Dad stood up and walked into the kitchen, then down the cellar stairs.

Mom started to move, and Tommy put his hand over hers.

"No," he said gently. "We're going to finish dinner. I cooked all last night for you. Let's not make a mole-hill into a mountain."

Then Lizzie's head poked around the corner. "Some molehill! Did he go?"

"He happens to be my husband, Lizzie," Mom said.

"Oh, honey, that's not your fault. Love is blind, Winnie, dear."

I felt sorry for Dad. I took him a plate of ham, potatoes, and cabbage, and another filled with animal cookies, springerles, and sandtarts, Pennsylvania Dutch specialties baked by Mom.

He was sitting in an old rocker with the springs busting from the bottom, not far from the black monster furnace with an appetite for coal second to no other. Around the back of the room were all the vegetables and fruits Mom had canned, and in the center was the work-bench with the jigsaw Dad and Bud had used when they'd made venetian blinds for every room in the house.

"Tommy told me you had a girlfriend, Jubal. Then he told me you didn't."

"I never really did, Dad."

"The little Daniel girl?"

"Daria. But she was never my girlfriend. We were just real close."

"And her father didn't approve, I bet."

"No. He didn't. You know Radio Dan. 'Slap your sides if you're off to war.'"

"I know Dan Daniel Senior. I know that he's a good man. We're all good men, Jubal. We're good, decent, God-fearing men. This war can't change that."

"Wasn't he one of the ones who snubbed you at Rotary?"

"Dan is my neighbor, on both the street where I live and the one where I work. We always say hello. We don't shake hands or have conversations anymore, but we certainly do what would be embarrassing for neighbors not to do."

"I don't think he's fit to polish Bud's shoes. That's how all this started. What did he ever do to make *him* so high and mighty?"

"He gave a son. What more can a man do?"

"You're mixing him up with God, Dad."

"Perhaps. . . . I wish someone would tell me why your aunt Lizzie feels she's been appointed to represent everyone on the planet who happens to be of the Jewish persuasion."

"I think she just gets enraged because no one in America seems to care what's happening to the Jews," I said. "At school we learned this country even refused a ship of Jewish refugees in 1940. We wouldn't even let Jews come in as temporary visitors."

Dad stabbed the ham with his fork. "Don't say Jews! It isn't polite," he said.

"We wouldn't let people of the Jewish persuasion even come in as temporary visitors. I read up on it, Dad. Lizzie's right about a lot of stuff!"

Dad wasn't going to argue.

He chewed his dinner for a while, then said, "I remember the summer you went to Cub Scout camp and Dean Daniel went home because he was afraid of spiders."

"I thought of the same thing, Dad."

"Well, he ran into something a lot more fear-inspiring than arachnids. Those filthy Japs got him! Filthy slant eyes got him!"

I'd never heard that kind of talk from my father. At SCFS we were taught to avoid name-calling, that war was no excuse to make the enemy seem different from us. We had to realize if we chose to go to war, we chose to kill people just like us.

"I remember that night at the Trenton station," Dad said.

"How did you feel that night, Dad?"

"Ashamed and embarrassed for myself, and for Bud." Dad shrugged his shoulders and sighed. "I couldn't help it."

"I think we all felt funny. Some Quakers."

"I'm nobody's Quaker. I just went along with your mother."

"I wish you'd be with her more now," I said. I'd never

said anything of the kind to him before, and I regretted it immediately. He gave me a look. Then he put his plate on the table beside him, got up, and went across to get the coal bucket and the shovel.

"Chilly in here," he said. "Go up and tell your mother that Hope called while you were at meeting. She's calling again tonight, between nine and ten."

"What a thrill!" I said, but Dad wasn't in a mood to kid around about Hope, as we used to. He wasn't buying any more intimacy. When I tried to take the coal shovel from his hand, he said, "Do as I told you, Jubal."

★ ★ ★

NINETEEN

C hristmas night Lizzie and Mom planned to play
Monopoly. Dad said he wanted to see exactly how
much he'd lost compared to last year. He'd wanted to
feature gala markdown sales, but what Quaker belief he
had left kept him from making something commercial
out of a celebration of the Lord's birth. All the other
merchants held holiday sales, and all seemed to have had
a banner year. But Dad's problem luring customers into
Shoemaker's had nothing to do with sales. He knew it,
and we knew it too. Still, no one was saying out loud
how badly Bud was hurting us.

Tommy was out with Rose Garten. He said whatever it was Hope wanted, he could hear about it the next
day. We always felt like postponing news from Hope,
fearing that our luck wouldn't last, that someday she
would be calling to announce she'd landed Bud. That was
how we thought of it, that she'd reel him in like a big
fish, ignoring the fact Bud was mad about her.

Christmas night The Teen Canteen was not only
open but showing *Yankee Doodle Dandy*. I remembered
Daria telling me how she'd loved that movie. It began at
six and it would be over in plenty of time for me to get
back home and find out Hope's news.

Tommy hadn't worn his new Christmas tie. A tie would only be in the way of Fast Tom that evening. It was this sharp dark-blue-and-white-striped number I decided to wear myself, with Bud's old blue blazer and his gray flannel pants. The pants were so old they had cuffs, a taboo since the war. I shined my loafers and polished the gold tie clip that was also Tommy's. I borrowed some of his Vitalis for my hair.

The Teen Canteen had been the Catholic church's answer to gas rationing and the seasonal closing of Chester Park. It gave kids a place to go their parents would okay. Older kids and servicemen went to the Side Door Canteen at City Hall.

But everyone was invited to the Teen Canteen movies, and Sweet Creek was full of people at loose ends that Christmas night, including a Marine and half a dozen sailors.

I sat on one of the folding chairs in the last row. That way I could see Daria if she came in. There were so many there for the show, they had to throw in some extra chairs.

The only thing I knew about the picture was that it was the life of George M. Cohan. I knew he was a songwriter and a dancer. I didn't know what songs he'd written.

No one from Sweet Creek Friends seemed to be there. Marty Allen had said he might show up, and I'd said if he did and Daria didn't, I'd hang around with him.

After the film got going, I wasn't surprised that I was probably the only Quaker present. It was all about good old war!

Daria hadn't come, of course. I knew that was just wishful thinking. What I didn't know was how to get out of there without climbing over people's knees. Even if I did manage that, how would I find my overcoat on the rack in back, in the dark?

So I sat there right to the last scene, a major tear-jerker. It took place outside the White House. Marching soldiers all singing "Over There." The people on the sidewalk were cheering and singing along with the soldiers: " . . . *the Yanks are coming, the drums rum-tumming everywhere—*" Suddenly across the White House lawn George M. Cohan came, played by Jimmy Cagney. All he could do was stand and look amazed, because he was so touched by them singing a song he'd written. A passing soldier stopped long enough to ask George what was the matter ("old-timer")—didn't he remember the song?

George nodded and said it seemed he did remember it.

Then George joined in the singing with the soldiers. He marched in step with them as the words grew louder. "AND WE WON'T COME BACK 'TIL IT'S OVER OVER THERE!"

"What's the matter, Shoemaker?" a voice asked. "What's your hurry?"

I had just found my overcoat when Luke Casper spoke to me.

"Nothing's the matter," I said.

"Great movie, hmmm?"

"Yeah."

"People tell me I look like him."

We were walking toward the exit. My heart was beating fast. It surprised me, still, when I reacted sentimentally to stuff about the war. It was hard not to react when there was music, marching, and American flags waving. I'd have a lump in my throat and an argument against it in my head.

Luke asked, "Do *you* think I look like James Cagney?"

"No," I said. But he did. His face did, a lot, although he was taller and huskier. I wasn't in the mood to flatter him.

"So what'd you really think of the movie?" he said.

"I liked the music."

"I didn't think you would," he said. "I thought it would be too patriotic for you."

"You know so much about me."

"I know you lost your girl."

I didn't answer that.

"She hasn't been by the stable in a long time," he said.

"Her brother died. Didn't you hear?"

"Oh, I heard. I wondered if you heard. I wondered how *you* felt when *you* heard. I wondered how your brother felt when *he* heard." Why hadn't I just *admitted* that he looked like James Cagney?

"Shut up, Luke."

"*You* shut up."

"Both of you shut up!" a sailor said. "You're in a church!"

"That's right!" from others.

I could see a priest hurrying toward us through the crowd. Another one was feeding slugs into the jukebox, while the Catholic Boys' Club stacked the chairs to clear the floor for dancing.

I pushed through the door, and Luke was right behind me.

"Hey, don't you want a ride home?"

"No, thanks."

"Shall I give her your love when I see her, Jubal?"

I kept on going.

"Because I'm going to see her!" Luke shouted. "No kidding!"

He liked to see if he could get me mad enough to fight. He'd say, "Jubal, I know you want to sock me in the kisser. What'll it take to make you try?"

On the walk home my heart felt like it would punch its way out of my chest. All I needed, on top of World War I, was Luke Casper. Luke Casper talking about seeing Daria. My mind spun back to the last afternoon Daria and I were together, when she'd told him he was a sweetheart and told me he looked like Cagney. Maybe he wasn't baiting me. What made me think she wouldn't go out with someone who looked like Jimmy Cagney?

When I got home, Mom, Lizzie, and Dad were in the living room. There was just one lamp lit, plus the light from the large Stromberg-Carlson radio/record player that had been sent from a local Sears, courtesy of Lizzie. The house was cold. Mahatma came slinking across the room with his head down, tail wagging between his legs, the way he looked sometimes when he'd done something wrong, or someone else had.

"We've been waiting for you. Is Tommy with you?" Mom asked.

"No. What's going on?" What I really meant was, What happened to bring Dad up from the cellar? What happened to make Dad put on a suit and tie at this hour of night?

"Hope called," Mom said. "Bud is in the hospital. He was very badly beaten up by an Indian patient."

"Sky Hawk," I said. *You should see the size of him!*

"He's in bad shape," Dad said.

"How bad?"

"Bad!" Lizzie said. "We're all going down there. Tonight!"

"I want to drive," said Dad, as though they'd been arguing the point. "We'll take *our* car."

Lizzie said, "My car if we're using my gas rationing tickets."

"Oh, Lizzie, you always have extra," Mom said.

"Don't ask where she gets them," said Dad.

"We save them, Efram, so I can spend time with my sister! Don't you dare insinuate we get them any other way!"

"We're taking the Buick," Dad said, "and we better get going."

Lizzie said, "We'll take the Lincoln. I'll drive."

"I want to go too!" I said.

"No," Mom said. "You and Tommy stay here."

"Please, Mom."

"You have to open the store," Dad said, never one to forget that.

They took the Buick, too.

★ ★ ★
TWENTY

Dear Jubal,

I am very sorry to learn about Bud, and I hope he will be all right. It is often the do-gooders that bad things happen to because you cannot change what is just by wishing it would change. I remember you telling me about that Indian.

Jubal, I want to turn over a new leaf in the new year, and this is another reason I am writing this letter. This letter needs no response, and I would appreciate it if you did not answer it.

I have to tell you something I did and I was wrong about it, though it was done with the best intentions. Like Bud, I misjudged the situation. Also I think I was a little crazy, you know, with both my brothers gone. I got the idea I could protest the CO thing marking your store windows. You thought I stopped after you found me out, but I didn't. I put the yellow Ys there. I even thought (this is how crazy I really was) that I had to do it because of seeing so much of you. I believed if I didn't, something would happen to Danny or Dean.

Jubal, this sounds nuts, I know, but I also talked Mom into getting rid of that casserole. I began to think anything connected with you was a jinx . . . that next Daniel could go.

It's funny that I really never thought it would be Dean, because he never described bad things. His letters kept coming after we knew he was dead, and he had written things like "In a broadcast today Tokyo Rose said we American soldiers were 'like summer insects that have dropped into the fire themselves.' Nice of her to wax poetic, don't you agree?"

Danny says he is not all that sure your brother is that off the mark, because try to name a war that wasn't caused by an earlier one and won't cause a future one. I'm not sure I agree with that or even understand it, but Danny says your family is probably guilty enough without me acting as judge and prosecutor.

What I am sorry about is not so much what I did to the windows (honest, I was just trying to express my opinion) but the lying to you, Jubal. How could I lie to the one person I looked forward to being with and began to consider my best friend?

I hope you will accept my apology.

Oh, Jubal, I miss you a bundle! There is nothing I can do about the way my father and mother feel. Maybe someday, when the winter has passed (if you can forgive me), I can sneak by the Harts' after my lesson. I miss Quinn, too. I miss us. But don't take this as a sign to call me. Daddy can't seem to forgive Bud. God only knows what he would say if he knew you feel the same way, or at least I assume you still do. I assume Dean's death didn't do anything to change your mind. That is the awful problem, Jubal. I miss you but not that part of you.

Your friend,
Daria

P.S. HAPPY NEW YEAR, JUBAL!

PART THREE

★ ★ ★

If you know about K-rations,
*   slap your sides,*
If you have a lot of patience,
*   slap your sides,*
If you know the onion smell
*   is to make our boys eat well,*
Slap your sides,
Cheer for Wride's,
Slap your sides!

Happy New Year, listeners!

"Moonlight Becomes You," Ensign Polliver, or so one of our Wride girls thinks. Her name's Lorelei Lewis and she's over at Wride Foods, on the first floor, winning the war. But I don't have to tell you where she is, Roger Polliver, United States Navy, U.S. of A.!

This song is dedicated to you from Lorelei.

—<u>Radio Dan broadcast, 1943</u>

★ ★ ★
TWENTY-ONE

"Happy New Year!" Rose Garten said. "This is the first time I've ever had real champagne."

"It's just my second time," I said. Tommy'd told me I could have only half a glass. He had to make the bottle last the whole night.

We were sitting at the dining-room table waiting for Tommy to serve a dessert called bananas Foster. He had found the recipe in a rum advertisement in *Esquire* magazine. He had bought a pony of Bacardi rum when he'd bought the champagne.

We had already finished a meat loaf, baked potatoes, and my mother's canned green beans.

My folks were still in Virginia with Bud.

I'd talked on the phone with him. He said not to worry about him, he'd be okay. But pray for the Indian. He was getting the blame for something he didn't do.

Rose was trying to get her parents on the telephone to ask if she could spend the night. An unexpected winter storm was covering Bud's old Ford with snow.

Tommy kept saying things like "I hope they don't think I'm going to risk our lives driving you back to Blooming Glen in *this* weather!"

"They won't like it that there's no one here."

"You're nineteen, Rose! You're no kid!"

"Tell *them* that."

"And my brother's here, for Pete's sake!" Tommy said.

"I don't think Jubal's their idea of a chaperone."

"Then don't tell them my parents aren't here."

"I already told them they were down with Bud."

"Well that was dumb!" Tommy said.

Tommy was at 85 on the graph. I knew he was counting on making 100 that night. He had already told me I was to announce that they had to disappear, right after they'd finished dessert, because *I* preferred to clear the table and do dishes by myself.

"You prefer to do dishes by yourself listening to our radio," Tommy coached me. "Don't sound like a martyr, or she'll jump up and say we'll all pitch in."

"Okay."

"And make it clear that you're going to be in bed at the stroke of midnight, that you like being in bed and listening to the excitement from Times Square on our radio."

"Why am I supposed to keep mentioning our radio?"

"So she doesn't think you expect to be listening to the Stromberg-Carlson with me and her."

"Okay," I said. "You're not going to take her up to the master bedroom, I hope?"

"Jubal, I'm a little more suave than *that*!"

"So where will you be?"

"In the living room! On the davenport!"

It was Tommy's idea that the two of us wear jackets and ties. He had bought Rose a gardenia corsage. He'd found a pair of green candles and shaved their ends so they could fit Coke bottles. He'd stripped two pieces of tinfoil from the huge ball Dad kept down in the basement for the war effort and wrapped them around the bottles. He'd cut out place cards for us: an angel for Rose, a star for me, a quarter moon for himself.

The Stromberg-Carlson was playing softly in the living room. Rose wore a red-velvet dress with a scoop neck and a strand of pearls to match her earrings. She had brown hair like Daria's, only Daria's was lighter, longer, softer.

I wished Daria could have been there. I thought of her all through dinner. I was answering her letter in my mind. I told her that Bud hadn't gotten hurt because he was a do-gooder. He'd gotten hurt because some locals went after him.

Bud had taken Sky Hawk to a movie in town. Afterward they'd hitched a ride home with the wrong truckful of rowdies. These hoodlums had called Bud a conchie and poured beer over Sky Hawk's jacket. The Indian had panicked and run, which was when they took turns holding and punching Bud. They'd told the police that liquor had made the Indian violent. The police had found Sky Hawk and booked him.

The bananas Foster arrived with blue flames over it. Tommy let Rose blow them out, and we all dug in.

"I suppose you still like to do the dishes all by yourself," Tommy said to me.

"Yes. I like to do them and listen to the radio."

"I never heard of a boy *liking* to do dishes," said Rose.

"We've got a new Zenith radio," Tommy said.

"I like to go to bed before the new year's rung in and listen to reports from all over the world," I said.

"Don't you listen to Radio Dan from right on Pilgrim Lane? He reads the list of last year's war dead. This year his own son will be on it!"

"Jubal likes to listen to all the stuff going on in Times Square," Tommy said.

"Speaking of being dead, my father's going to kill me if I'm not home when I said I'd be," Rose said. "Or he's going to kill *you*, Tommy."

"Try calling them again," Tommy said. "I'll talk to him. . . . What kind of guy does he think I am?"

"A regular guy." Rose laughed.

While I did the dishes, I heard Tommy calling her father "Mr. Garten, sir." He told him that the three of us were going to make popcorn and listen to all the excitement from Times Square. He said we'd probably play a game of Monopoly, too. Rose, he said, can sleep in my parents' room, sir. We boys will sleep downstairs.

Then he crowed, "Yes, sir! . . . First thing in the morning, as soon as I shovel out!"

The snow was already up to the back porch.

I was finishing the dishes, toying with the idea of taking a chance and calling Daria, when the phone rang.

"Guess who wants to wish you Happy New Year!" said

Lizzie. She had gone back to New York from Virginia. Her Lincoln was in our garage, where she had decided it would stay all winter.

"Happy New Year, Aunt Liz."

"Someone wants to wish you Happy New Year, Jubal. Presenting Yeoman Natalia Granger. Your cousin is a Wave!"

Tommy was standing in his stocking feet at the edge of the living room. "I'm not here!" he whispered.

"Natalia's a Wave," I whispered back with my hand over the mouthpiece.

"I'm busy," he hissed. "I'm not here."

"Tommy's not here," I said.

"Hi, Jubal," Natalia said. "I didn't want my mother to tell you. I wanted to tell you myself. That was why I was dieting, too."

"Hi, Natalia. Thanks for the books."

"You're welcome. The Fitzgerald is the important one." I figured that was code for the dirtiest.

"Okay," I said. "How do you *like* the Waves?"

"She likes doing something for her country." Lizzie was on the extension.

"I love the Waves," Natalia said. "I'm in boot camp."

"Where is boot camp?"

"At Hunter College, here in New York. . . . Where's your handsome brother?"

"Tommy's not here," I said.

"The radio said it's snowing hard up there. Is the Lincoln in the garage?" Lizzie said.

After Natalia got off the extension, Mike got on. He said that Bud had had a narrow escape, and that Tommy and I should tell him not to pursue it.

"Not to pursue what?"

"Let the police charge the Indian," Mike said. "Otherwise Bud's going to be in deep *merde*."

"He'd never let them blame the Indian if the Indian didn't do it," I said.

"The Indian's in for it anyway," said Mike. "He tried to run away. Bud will just make things worse if he goes after the locals."

"*They* went after *him*," I said.

Lizzie said, "I don't agree with Mike, Jubal."

"When did you ever agree with me?" Mike said.

When I hung up, I saw that I'd forgotten the dessert dishes.

I tried to walk quietly. I could hear the radio playing softly in the living room.

After I pushed Mahatma out into the storm to do his business and come right back in, I went upstairs.

I turned on the radio and opened *Tender Is the Night*, ready to read the good parts. Instead, Natalia had marked a speech made by the hero, a psychiatrist called Dick Diver. He was visiting an old World War I battlefield with friends. He was describing war as a "love battle"—*not love of country, but love of a way of life, intense enough to cause men to risk their lives for it.*

In a handwriting that looked exactly like Lizzie's,

Natalia had written in a margin, "Jubal, don't you feel this yet? I do."

I thought of asking her what kind of love battle destroyed major cities like Cologne, Stalingrad, and London. Did it make sense risking your life to kill innocent civilians?

But nothing I said would change Natalia's mind, particularly now that she was Yeoman Granger.

I had myself to change, too. I wasn't as strong as I'd need to be if the war was still going on in three years. I remembered Christmas night, the tears behind my eyes when the soldiers were singing "Over There," at the same time I knew Hollywood was doing its best to make war look manly and moral and patriotic. I'd ask myself questions like When you witness, do you cheer your country's military victories in battles you refused to be a part of? You could lie to yourself that you were only cheering what could lead to the end of the war. But how could you root for our side? When it came to killing civilians, we were as guilty as they were.

I knew I wasn't the only one going to sleep nights asking myself things like that. There were rumors that even among Lancaster Mennonites, men took the 1AO classification without the church expelling them now. At SCFS we'd stopped a lot of our classroom discussion about witnessing. There were too many kids with relatives who were choosing to be 1A, not even 1AO. My friend Marty Allen now wanted to join up.

"Don't be mad, Jubal," he'd said. "It's something I have to do!"

He had to wait until he was seventeen.

"I won't be mad," I told him. "For certain Quakers I think it takes more guts to be 1A."

"How about you, Jubal?" Marty said. "You must have thought about it."

"I didn't," I said. "I don't."

"You want some advice?"

"That depends."

He gave me some anyway. "Stop trying to be Bud."

"Do you think that's all there is to it, Marty?"

"I know there's more. But I know you're not a fanatic. No one can be 4E in this kind of war who isn't a fanatic!"

I didn't tell Marty about my last phone conversation with Bud. He still had broken bones from being beat up, and he was looking into volunteering for some kind of starvation research. He was still gung ho.

At Friends even the teachers weren't talking a lot, anymore, about registering 4E. The focus had switched to what Friends would do *after* the war, how we would help the victims heal, help them find their way back to their cities, and help rebuild their homes. We'd done that after World War I, and we'd do it again.

I didn't wait to hear the New Year being rung in on the radio that night. I'd even forgotten to tune in to Radio Dan. Or maybe I forgot to remember on purpose. I didn't want to hear names of Sweet Creekers who wouldn't be around anymore, boys a few grades ahead of me, who'd been in Scouts with Bud.

I also forgot to say my prayers, and I fell asleep with all my clothes on. But I dreamed I was naked and I was downtown on Pilgrim Lane, my hands covering me in front, people pointing at me and laughing.

When I woke up, the sun was streaming into the room, and I could hear Fast Tom trying to get the Ford started.

★ ★ ★

TWENTY-TWO

Some afternoons I timed Mahatma's walks so my chances of seeing Daria were better. The Daniels went into their dining room every afternoon at five sharp, since Radio Dan had to be at WBEA at six thirty. Between four forty-five and five I would often be able to see Daria at the piano or the desk in the living room, waiting for her mother to put dinner on the table.

Tommy was wise to me and asked me if I didn't think I'd become pathetic. If I *was* pathetic, and I probably was, he'd been obnoxious ever since New Year's Eve. He had finally hit 100 on his graph. It was the finishing touch to what Tommy viewed as "manhood." He dressed almost always in a suit and tie, except when he was at the Harts' helping with the horses. Even there he sported a new pair of black jodhpurs and black riding boots. He cooked wearing a white apron and white chef's hat, and he often served the kinds of desserts that came from the kitchen aflame. My father would simply sit there shaking his head, wincing. I could remember when Dad had liked a little drama, some fun. There was the day, when I was very young, that Bud and his buddies put a cow in the meetinghouse. As people arrived, it was standing there, regarding them. Dad had tried to stop laughing long enough to bawl Bud out, once he discovered Bud was part of it.

Ever since Dad had come back from Virginia, he'd been crabby and suspicious. He even believed what the local police down there believed: that Bud was beaten up by the Indian. . . . They claimed Bud was this bleeding heart who'd misjudged the Indian's killer nature and taken him out of a locked ward to a movie in town! According to them, Bud was lucky the other customers hadn't been hurt.

Although Tommy's relationship with Rose was off and on (off nights she did not want the same thing he did), they were considered a couple in Sweet Creek. For the Valentine's ball held at Wride Them Cowboy she had been voted Queen of Hearts by the employees of Wride Foods, and Tommy had reigned beside her as the King.

That March a lot of the kids at SCFS were angry because 800 Flying Fortresses had dropped 2,000 tons of bombs on Berlin. Then we'd dropped 3,500 on Monte Casino. Somehow it was always worse when America was part of the mass destruction, never mind what was done to us or what the Russians did. How about when 100,000 Germans surrendered at Sevastopol, and were killed by our sweet allies? I'd done a paper about it, earning this comment from my teacher, Mrs. Kruppenberger: "Jubal, war is a lot like nose picking. Nobody does it in an acceptable way. It's better not to do it at all."

* * *

March seemed more like April, warmer, and becoming green. I took Tyke up on the trails near Chester Park. I was beginning to think of him as my only buddy.

Mr. Hart had Quinn out. He was saying his goodbye to him, as all of us were, one way or the other. I'd groom him the next day. His owner was taking him home.

Tyke had grown fond of Quinn, just as I had grown fond of Tyke. I rode Tyke about forty minutes every day, and I told him everything on my mind. I remember that particular March day very well, because I was telling Tyke I wished I could see Daria. Then, in the unbelievable way things happen sometimes, she was right at the bottom of the hill.

I whispered, "Hey! Tyke! There she is!"

She had stopped on the path that wound down from the Ochevskys' and led to the bus stop. She was watching me ride toward her.

I'd never seen the coat before. It was a brown shade matching her hair. A bright-yellow scarf around her neck. Brown boots with fur tops. I took it all in, the way you try to hang on to your dream when you first wake up because it slips away so fast. But she stood there, and she began waving. There was a grin across her face when we got to her.

I swung down off Tyke.

We said these fast hello-how-are-yous, and she asked me almost immediately how Bud was doing. I told her he'd been transferred to Welfare Island, New York.

He was entering an experimental medical program there, sponsored by the CPS.

"Is he well enough after that Indian attacked him?" Daria asked.

"He's not in top shape, but neither are a lot of people when they have to go without food. It's an experiment that has to do with how long starving victims can go without eating."

"Bud's very brave, isn't he . . . in his own way."

I said, "He's very brave no matter how you look at it."

"Okay," she said softly.

I told her the Indian hadn't attacked Bud, but no one chose to believe that down there. Sky Hawk was charged with the beating despite Bud's sworn statements to the contrary. But I didn't tell her Hope's theory: that Bud had volunteered for a study of starvation because he felt guilty about Sky Hawk. I didn't tell her that the beating had cost Bud most of the hearing in one ear. . . . All that sort of thing seemed irrelevant since Dean had been killed.

"And I hear your mother's working in the store now," said Daria.

"Not every day." It had been Mom's idea that the female customers might not want males waiting on them when they purchased certain things. I think Mom also thought some of the old customers would come back because of her.

It was too soon to tell.

My father wished she would not be there *any* day.

He never came right out and said so. He never came right out and said anything anymore.

"I miss riding Quinn," Daria said. She smelled like summer flowers, and I wondered if she was wearing the Evening in Paris I'd given her.

"Quinn's owner is taking him back tomorrow." I said.

"He *can't!*"

"Quinn is his. The Army's discharged him and he's back on his farm, in bad shape. He can't wait to see Quinn."

"I wish I could have one more ride. I wish *we* could go out together."

"Tomorrow's Saturday. I won't trailer him until around three."

"You don't know how badly I want to do it, Jubal."

"Then do it."

"And break a promise to my dad?"

"I'm not going to get into that. You have to make up your own mind."

"I'm afraid of Luke. He's gotten friendly with Dad. He drops off hamburgers, doughnuts, at the station, looking for me, I think. Someone at WBEA had to tell him my songs were recorded."

"That creep!"

"I'm afraid he'd tell Dad I was with you, just to get in good with him."

"You could see Quinn *now*. I don't think he's on much of a ride. Mr. Hart only takes him for about twenty minutes."

"I better not. Daddy gets upset when I don't come right home."

Tyke was nudging my neck.

"Look how he loves you, Jubal."

"I know."

"I almost love you myself sometimes," she teased. "Did you know that?"

"'All or nothing at all.'" I sang the opening of Sinatra's big hit.

She joined in: "'Half a love nev-ver appealed to me.'"

She smiled. "Say good-bye to Quinn for me, Jubal. I can't make it. I'm sorry."

"So am I. For you."

"I didn't mean I just wanted to ride Quinn a last time."

"That's how it sounded."

"But that isn't what I meant. . . . I miss you an awful lot, Jubal."

I had to look away and get control. Just her saying that made me want to bawl, made me want to cry out, *Me, too!* and grab her. But there we stood with the huge sentinel crows cawing above us on the gnarled limbs of the buttonwoods. There we stood.

"Yeah, I miss you, too," I finally managed.

"Sometimes I think it wasn't right for me to scold you about Bud. Or about your own feelings. You have a right to your opinions."

"That isn't the way I remember you, anyway."

"In his letters Daniel sometimes sounds more like you than you do."

We stood there a silent moment before she asked, "How *do* you remember me?"

"I remember how you used to suddenly sing something from a song . . . or an opera. The way we just sang out a second ago."

"I can't do it on command," she said.

"I'm not commanding you."

"I know that. . . . Do you listen to Daddy?"

"Sometimes." I don't know why I didn't just say Almost every night.

"He's got this new theme song. He's using the old one too, but I recorded a new one for him to play. And guess what—I wrote it."

"So now you're a writer, too."

"No, I did it for the girls at Wride's. It just came to me."

"Uh-huh. Good."

"So you can hear *that* if you ever catch the program."

"Okay."

"Oh, Jubal."

"What?"

"Just get back up on Tyke, hmmm? Just ride away."

"If that's what you want."

She didn't say it was or it wasn't. She turned in the other direction and walked away.

"I love her," I told Tyke on the way back to the stables.

His ears were pricked forward. He'd been acting strange lately, bolting his feed, pacing in his stall. I thought he sensed Quinn was leaving. Luke said that was what it was. Luke said horses felt plenty that we didn't know about.

"They're not that different from us," he said. "They intuit things."

★ ★ ★

TWENTY-THREE

Both Tommy and I took the day off to drive Quinn up past Lancaster. Mom would be at the store helping Dad.

As capable a man as Luke was with horses when he was sober, he wasn't ever the right one to trailer them. He didn't have the patience to load them. They sensed he didn't, and horses never help you when they find you out. Luke also drove too fast, always. A horse would be back there in the trailer trying to keep its balance.

I'd bathed and groomed Quinn on the day we were taking him. Across the stable Tyke had begun the pacing again, plus giving an occasional snort and neigh.

I was glad to get on the road earlier than we'd planned.

"I think Tyke knew Quinn was leaving. He's been so nervous."

"Maybe Tyke doesn't like being alone with Luke," said Tommy. "Would you? He stinks from booze, and it's only eleven thirty."

"Tyke's almost the way he used to be when he first came to us. Back when he was Ike."

"Mr. Hart's not too happy about the horse business," Tommy said. He'd had coffee with him while I was getting Quinn ready.

"Mr. Hart's not too happy period," I said.

"What's he got to be happy about? You've *never* been sympathetic toward Abel, have you?"

"I can't call myself a fan of his, no. But I wasn't even thinking about Abel. I just hope Mr. Hart doesn't give up the horses."

"Not you, too," Tommy said. "First we had Bud mad about Quinn. Now we've got you crazy about Tyke."

Quinn returned to a thirty-acre farm with an immaculate stable and large pastures, trails, and paddocks. His owner was on crutches, in mufti except for an Army cap, a big smile on his face. He was waiting for us in the driveway. After we backed Quinn out, and Quinn saw where he was and who was there to greet him, Quinn showed off. We'd never seen him prance around the way he did, high-stepping and nickering.

On the way back Tommy said, "Bud will be relieved when we tell him about taking Quinn home."

"I don't know. Do we want Bud to know Quinn's *that* happy without him?"

We had the radio playing loud, the way we both liked it. We listened to Sinatra and Harry James and Dinah Shore.

"Do you think Mom and Dad are ever going to be the way they used to be?" I asked Tommy.

"I have no idea. Neither one will talk about it."

Tommy had this new celluloid black eyeshade he liked to wear. He was wearing the black jodhpurs and one of the white shirts Mom ironed for him every day. The black boots. He looked like a combination card shark and plantation owner.

"We're not a family that talks much about things," I said.

"*We* talk about things," he said. "Don't we?"

"Sometimes . . . but I had to sneak a look at Bud's letter to get you to talk about that. Remember?"

"I remember. And you sneak peeks at my graphs."

"Because you don't talk about it."

"What if I did?" Tommy said.

"Okey-dokey, go right ahead," I said.

"Things aren't so okey-dokey, Jubal."

"You mean with Rose?"

"That's what I mean. Oh, gawd!" he groaned.

"What's the matter?"

"She's got herself in trouble," he said.

"How?"

"She's got herself pregnant," he said.

"You mean *you* did. What are you going to do?"

"I wish she could get rid of it."

"She can't get rid of it, Tommy!"

"I'm not saying she can. I'm saying I wish she could."

"Even if there was someplace to take her, and even if there was some way to afford it, she's Catholic."

"Don't *you* remind me. She reminds me enough."

"You're going to have to marry her," I said.

"I don't love her," Tommy said. That was our only subject on the way back to Doylestown.

"If I marry Rose, it will ruin my life," Tommy said.

"What about hers?"

"I know. It would ruin hers also, but she'd have the baby, anyway."

"You'd have the baby too!"

"I don't *want* the baby! What do you think I'm talking about?"

"I feel sorry for her, Tommy. She's crazy about you."

"Girls love being mothers. She'd have the baby. I'd have the bills. I'd have her old man showing me his bowling trophies. . . . I'd never go on a date again. That part of my life would be over—pffft!"

"Did you *ever* love her?"

"I don't know."

"Did you *say* you loved her?"

"You *say* it. You *always* say it. If you don't say it, they won't do it."

"You never should have said it."

"I never should have done it!"

Tommy didn't want to take the time to stop for lunch at a road stand. He wanted to go home and meet with the coach at Sweet Creek High School. He said that besides Bud, the coach was the only adult he trusted. He didn't want to lay it on Bud. Bud had his own problems.

Back at the Harts', Tommy slammed the car door and said, "Don't tell anyone what I just told you!"

"Don't worry."

"Are you going to help me clean the trailer?"

"Let Luke do it. Let him do something for a change."

"He's probably too loaded by now."

"I want to ride Tyke."

"Go on then, but remember what I said. Don't tell anyone!"

"Who would I tell?"

"Just zip the lip, Jubal!"

I was walking up toward the stables, feeling sorry for myself. I was hungry, too, and angry. There was no way Tommy could get out of marrying Rose. Even forgetting the fact that her father was a carbon copy of Attila the Hun, any boy in Sweet Creek who got a girl in trouble had to have the proverbial shotgun wedding. . . . I was cussing to myself. It suddenly dawned on me that I would be the only child living at home. I would be the only person my mother would be able to talk to and the only person my father would be able to talk to. But I wouldn't know how to really talk with either one of them. I'd always had Bud or Tommy.

At first I thought the cry I heard was one of the stable cats in heat. Then I realized it was a girl crying. She was crying, "Help!"

It was someone in trouble.

I began to run. I thought of Luke, thought of him drunk, and then when the voice called, "Help me!" I knew the voice.

"Daria! I'm coming!"

Scare him off, I thought. "*We're* coming!" I shouted, even though I'd looked behind me and didn't see Tommy anywhere.

I had never run so fast. I had never known I *could* run so fast. A powerful rush of rage and adrenaline drove me.

Again she cried out, "Please, some—" and the rest of what she'd said was muffled by what? Luke's hand across her mouth?

I headed straight for the stable door.

Just outside it I saw the pitchfork stuck in the block of hay.

★ ★ ★
TWENTY-FOUR

Hello, listeners. This is Radio Dan, your Home Front Man, bringing you the war . . . and tonight bringing you some thoughts about what's happened here in Sweet Creek that's put us on the map, sad to say not in a glowing light.

And you all know, so I'm not going to pretend you don't—you all know that my Darie is a part of this story . . . a very important part.

I've never spent any time with this young man the tabloid journalists enjoy calling the Quaker Killer. His father and I have been colleagues and neighbors for some twenty years. And I know many of you have done your shopping in Shoemaker's on Pilgrim Lane, and come to know Efram and Winnie.

Many of you know they belong to Sweet Creek Friends. The fact that they are Quakers is no small part of this story. Many of you are aware, too, that their oldest boy, Bud, chose to be a conscientious objector. In 1942 Bud entered Civilian Public Service.

Another, son, Thomas, attempted to join the Army and was rejected because of a perforated eardrum.

Now we come to Jubal.

I'm told by Darie that Jubal was planning to follow

in Bud's footsteps. Jubal, Darie told me, is a bona fide pacifist, a Quaker with strong convictions, a young man of fifteen who had already made up his mind that he was *not* going to participate in a war, in a fight of any kind, in violence.

You know, we parents think our kids tell us most things. Sure, they keep some things to themselves. But if you had a daughter and she had a regular date with a fellow, to go riding up to Chester Park most Saturday afternoons, wouldn't she tell her dad, or her mom, or someone?

She did tell someone. Darie Daniel told two people, in fact: her twin brothers. And when Dean was killed, she kept right on describing to Daniel the happy times she spent on horseback with Jubal Shoemaker.

The reason she couldn't confide in her old man, yours truly, or her mother, was that we aren't very sympathetic with Bud Shoemaker's position on the war . . . and we wouldn't have liked Jubal's pacifism any better.

Why, the only one my wife and yours truly could think of who had a *worse* attitude about this war was a man named Abel Hart. Abel Hart, draft resister, escaped convict, mental case . . . Yes, he is from our area, too. Or he *was*. From Doylestown.

Here's the thing, listeners; here's the thing.

My Darie believed she had a date to go riding with young Shoemaker, the pacifist. She went over to the Harts' stable in Doylestown to meet him.

Now, he wasn't there. There'd been a misunderstanding. He was on his way there, but he wouldn't arrive for a few minutes.

Someone was there, however. He'd been there off and on for about a week. It is said that one of the horses, named after General Dwight D. Eisenhower, was upset over it. This horse, Ike, was pacing and bolting his feed because he knew someone was hiding there in the straw . . . hiding from the law, the war, himself . . . even though by all rights he did live there. It was his home there. He was Abel Hart. . . . Maybe he didn't know who he was anymore, but he knew enough to find his way home and hide.

My Darie didn't recognize him. Nobody would have. I don't think his own father would have. Abel's hair had turned white and was down past his shoulders. He was in old, torn clothes reeking of filth. His hands had long nails and were all curled into claws. The ironic thing is I doubt that he meant Darie any harm. It was just that when she saw him, she began to scream, and he was afraid she would give him away. He put his hand over her mouth and muttered that he had the eyes of God now.

Well . . . Oh, listeners, the world is filled with irony. It is filled with drama. Here is a young man, fifteen, a Quaker, and something else about him: He was besotted with my Daria. This shy young man, this well-meaning young man (forget his pacifist leanings) spent five dollars and change on perfume for my daughter at Christmas. Evening in Paris, it was called. She wasn't even seeing that much of him anymore, but he couldn't get her off of his mind.

That fatal Saturday he heard her cry from outside the Hart stables. He believed that she was in danger—she may very well have been. Here was a crazy person who was telling her he saw with God's eyes. Here was a crazy person saying that to my daughter, and putting his large hand over her mouth, this smelly lunatic! My Darie was terrified! My Darie, in the dark of the Hart stable, had never been so afraid.

UNTIL.

Until, listeners, the pacifist came through the door bearing a pitchfork. The Quaker, the peacemaker, the shy, young fifteen-year-old member of Sweet Creek Friends School found something out about himself.

He found out that he COULD kill.

He found out that he WOULD kill.

In the few minutes it took to sense that someone he loved could be threatened, years and years of pacifist propaganda went down the tubes.

No one was going to hurt his girl!

Whoever tried to hurt his girl, was—*pfffft*—slap your sides—*slain!*

Food for thought, is it not listeners?

Tonight I've given you something to think about . . . and Jubal Shoemaker has given me something to think about. . . . I still don't want that boy anywhere near my Darie, but . . . I thank God for that boy. I pray to God that Jubal Shoemaker will not be punished too severely for being more of a man than he ever dreamed he was!

Good night, my faithful listeners.

And again tonight we're going to go out with my Darie singing her tribute to the home-front girls—you know their names as well as I do.

> *Rich gal, she wears the best perfume,*
> *Po' gal, she'd like to do the same,*
> *Wride gal got an onion smell,*
> *And that's why she's my dame!*
>
> *Rich gal, she lives in a big white house,*
> *Po' gal she lives in a frame,*
> *Wride gal got an onion smell*
> *And one room down the lane.*
>
> *Wride gal, you are swell,*
> *And you, gal, I adore,*
> *Wride gal, you pitched in*
> *To help us win this war!*
>
> *Wride gal, Wride gal,*
> *You helped us win this war!*

—<u>Radio Dan broadcast, 1944</u>

TWENTY-FIVE

"Daria?"

"Jubal?"

Penn Station, New York City, August 1945. One year and five months since I'd seen her.

"Where are you going?" she said, as though she was surprised to see me out of Sweet Creek. Everyone knew I got a suspended sentence, providing I didn't leave Sweet Creek for sixteen months.

It was my first time away from home since March 1944.

I had to do public service too, and another provision of my sentence was that I was to refrain from contact of any kind with Daria.

"Oh, Jubal! What a good surprise to see you here!"

"Yeah. It is a good surprise."

"What are you doing in the big city?"

"I'm visiting Bud."

"Bud's here too?"

"He's still with CPS, and still on Welfare Island. He's coming in for lunch."

"How long has it been since we've seen each other, Jubal?"

"Search me," I said. A century. A millennium. I tried

to look into her eyes, but she glanced at mine only a second.

"I'm sorry about your father," she said.

"His heart was real bad."

My dad had died four months earlier, the day after President Roosevelt did. He fell over in our kitchen, raging against Truman—against the idea of someone like himself, "a haberdasher," running the country in the middle of a war.

I'd find myself saying his heart was bad whenever anyone gave me condolences. I think I was pretending that it was *just* his heart, and not any aggravation I'd caused him.

"Thanks for your sympathy card, Daria." She'd picked out that tacky card that said someone wasn't dead, someone was just away. But she'd written underneath the verse,

I will never, ever forget you, ever!

Those seven words stayed with me. I'd tell myself she didn't *have* to write that.

"Tell Bud hello," she said.

"I will. Is Daniel home yet?"

"That's why I'm on my way to Sweet Creek. Dan's finally on leave."

She put her suitcase down a moment and took off the yellow sailor hat she was wearing. She'd let her brown hair grow past her shoulders.

"How do you like boarding school?" I deliberately

didn't say Farleigh Hall because I didn't want to give her the impression I was keeping track of her.

"Fine, and I'm back at Camp Rainbow this summer."

"Can you ride there? Do they have horses?"

"I can, and I do . . . but it's not the same."

"Nothing is," I said.

"No, nothing is, really."

I wasn't walking Mahatma by her house and trying to see in her windows anymore, times I knew she was probably home on vacation. I wasn't even asking about her, but I'd listen around and I'd hear. I'd known she was at the camp for kids with polio for the third summer. I knew Farleigh Hall was near Princeton, New Jersey.

I wrote down where she was on the back of my calendar.

My calendar had a record of my public service, stuff I had to do instead of serving time. Pick up trash at Chester Park weekend mornings, and some nights I sat at court to check in drunks, wife beaters, and teenage roughnecks. Every day after school I cleaned the latrines at City Hall.

I never went to the Harts' again.

Mr. Hart called personally to tell me he knew his son's death was an accident. He bore no grudge, he told me, and I was welcome, either to work or visit. But I couldn't go there, not even to see Tyke. Luke wasn't over there anymore either. He'd left for a job in Cumberland County.

* * *

Daria had on a yellow cotton dress, and those high heels called spectators. It was the pumps that made her seem taller than I was. I remembered when I used to worry that I was short.

"I'm glad I left Sweet Creek," she said.

"I didn't know you were that unhappy there."

"I wasn't, up until the trouble," she said. "Now I can't stand it! I hated what the newspaper wrote about us, as though we were an item."

I tried to remember if I had ever believed the same thing, or if she had *always* let it be known that she didn't feel that way about me.

"Your father made it clear it was all one-sided," I said. "He didn't waste any time shipping you off to school, either."

"I think he really *believed* he was getting me out of harm's way, you know what I mean?"

"I guess."

"I don't mean you in particular."

"I know."

"I've never in my life been so scared as I was that day Abel jumped out at me! . . . Thank God for you, Jubal! I know I never thanked you."

"That's okay."

She gave a defeated little laugh and put her hat back on.

"How's Tommy?" she asked.

"He's fine. He and Rose and the baby have been

living with us since Dad died."

"I heard. They were real brave to just stay in Sweet Creek and not give a hoot what anyone said!"

"They gave a hoot. Particularly Rose. But I don't think they had much choice, Daria."

She was frowning and still avoiding my eyes. I think she felt obligated to say something, to somehow make more of this chance meeting.

I said, "I'm late, so—"

She looked relieved. "So . . . so long, Jubal." She touched the sleeve of my pinstripe seersucker suit with her long fingers.

"So long," I said.

I didn't wait and watch her walk away.

I asked for directions to Grand Central Terminal, and I rode the subway with my heart pounding.

Someday, I believed, she wouldn't have that effect on me. But our lives would always be linked, no matter what became of me.

If it had been Luke Casper menacing Daria, and if it had been Luke Casper I had killed, I would surely have stood trial. I probably would have served time for manslaughter.

But it was a relief to almost everyone that Abel had been destroyed, whether it was willful on my part or the accident it had been.

I'd pleaded guilty before a judge who was later one of my father's pallbearers. A fellow Rotarian. He was a friend of Radio Dan's. I always believed he'd been instructed by Daria's father to include staying away from her as part of my punishment.

"Do you have anything to say for yourself, Jubal Shoemaker?" he'd asked.

"All my life I'll wish I could take back the day I killed Abel Hart," I said.

"What about if he really *had* been about to do harm to Miss Daniel?"

"Could I have stopped him without killing him? I think so, but I didn't try."

Before I'd crushed Abel's spine with the pitchfork, I'd heard the bone crack, heard him yelp like some miserable, abused street dog. He was too weak and defeated to make a louder noise.

"Don't keep talking about it, Jubal," Bud said. I'd met him across the street from Grand Central Terminal, in a large restaurant called Longchamps. "Don't beat yourself up about it."

"I hardly ever talk about it," I said. "It's just that we've never really discussed it."

"It's not your fault."

"You know that I never meant to kill him! I couldn't even see him in the dark! I thought it was Luke!"

"I know, Jube."

"I grabbed that pitchfork to threaten Luke, to make him stop whatever he was doing to Daria! I thought Luke was drunk. I didn't intend to kill *anyone*."

"It's hard for you because you never liked Abel."

"And people are talking about that, too. I know they are."

There were even kids at SCFS who thought that I wouldn't have been able to kill just anyone . . . that I must have hated Abel . . . and there were those who could remember I'd called him names and made fun of him. No one had ever heard me speak against Luke. No one knew anything about Daria and me or that I resented the way Luke behaved around her.

Bud said, "People in Sweet Creek aren't talking about you. You did them a favor! Abel's out of sight, out of mind. If they had their way, we'd *all* be out of sight permanently. Not just for the duration."

He took his hearing aid out of his ear and tapped it against the table. Hope had told Mom that he was always imagining there was something wrong with the equipment, but the truth was, he was getting deafer.

Bud still didn't care what he wore. He looked like he'd grabbed what he had on from that bin down at the soup kitchen. His jacket sleeves ended way above his wrists, and the collar of his sport shirt was frayed. Plus he looked like something out of a concentration camp. The experiment was over, but he was having trouble gaining the weight back, because he'd become a vegetarian.

Lizzie'd started calling him Saint Bud. She'd make the sign of the cross when she'd say his name.

At Longchamps I ate chicken chow mein while he had a Welsh rarebit. He showed me some pictures of

Hope. She'd written me to say Abel never would have survived, anyway. His mind was gone.

It should have helped to be told that, but it didn't stop me from hearing the crack of that bone, and the high little cry from Abel's throat. It didn't stop me from knowing that with one thrust I'd killed someone as defenseless as a frightened animal.

I had photographs, too, at lunch that day.

I passed them to Bud one by one.

"It's hard to look at family photos and not see Dad," he said.

Dad scowling, I thought to myself, but I didn't say it. Between the two of us we had probably hastened Dad's death. But Bud had never seen him near the end, when he'd forgotten how to smile, when he sulked down in the cellar—the hell with Mom, the hell with us all.

"This is all we need, Jubal!" Dad had declared when the police brought me home from the Harts' that day.

What none of our family had foreseen was the feeling of relief in the community. It was easier to understand someone who'd kill than it was to understand someone who wouldn't. The Shoemakers were just like everyone else after all. Bud was a maverick, an embarrassment, and because of Bud our business still suffered. But my mother got letters from people in Sweet Creek who wanted her to know they understood what she was going through because of what I'd done. And my father took a perverse glee in the idea of my devout mother suffering this homicide in the family. There was a new spring to his step, and he was snide and smug.

Bud passed the photos back to me.

"Poor Tommy," he said. "He still tries to dress like Fast Tom, doesn't he? Lookit that white jacket with the navy pants!"

"Rose spoils him," I said. "She buys him clothes. She's on the night shift at Wride's now, and she makes more than Tommy does. But he comes home to have lunch with her and Garten everyday."

"Garten Shoemaker. That's quite a moniker for a little guy."

"It's her maiden name."

"I know. . . . What's she like?"

"Lizzie says there's just one word for Rose. Pleasant."

"Lizzie likes to nail everyone, doesn't she?" Bud took a Camel from his pack and lit it. He said, "How's the store doing?"

"Thanks to Radio Dan, we're almost back to normal. He plugs Winnie's Weekly Winner. It was his idea for Mom to feature something every week."

"What about his daughter?"

I wasn't going to tell him we'd just run into each other at Penn Station. I didn't want Bud to pick at it. I doubted I'd tell anyone.

I said, "She's around."

"Are you still hung up on her?"

"I got over that."

"Because if you're going to witness, it helps to have a girl who's supportive."

"Yeah . . . but don't you think the war's winding down?"

"Like it was winding down at the end of *All Quiet on the Western Front*?" Bud gave me one of his sardonic smiles. "How many people will be killed, do you think, while the war's winding down?"

The same day I arrived back in Sweet Creek, an American B-29 bomber, *Enola Gay*, dropped an atomic bomb over the city of Hiroshima, a port on Japan's eastern coast. The bomb was called Little Boy, and the haberdasher running the country in the middle of a war pronounced it "the greatest thing in history!"

Three days later a second bomb, named Fat Man, was dropped on one of Japan's innermost cities, Nagasaki.

Bud was right to wonder how many people would be killed before the war wound down. Some 210,000 Japanese were known to be dead just because of Little Boy and Fat Man.

That fall our teachers at SCFS talked of a whole new concept of war in which fighting men would never be needed in such numbers again . . . in which there would be no draft. What would become of protests against war, when the means to wage it had been so profoundly changed? We had many debates. And when peace came, we had plans. A majority of our seniors signed up with the American Friends Service Committee, to do relief work in Europe before going on to college. I was one of them.

Soon after the Japanese surrendered unconditionally aboard the USS *Missouri*, in Tokyo Bay, Radio Dan made an announcement.

Listeners, this is your old home-front pal Radio Dan. I'm moving on now. They say in the Bible there's a time to reap and a time to sow and so forth and so on, and I'm adding my thought that there's a time to move on.

I've been invited to have a little show up in the Finger Lakes, in a peaceful little hamlet called Auburn, New York.

My wife, and Darie, and my son, Daniel, went there with me for a looksee, and we liked what we saw. I think Darie and Daniel like the idea of the illustrious Cornell University being right nearby . . . "Far above Cayuga's waters." . . . Oh, yes.

Now our wonderful sponsors, the Wrides, are closing their plant. No more K-rations (do I hear a cheer from the troops at that news?), so no more onions. Breathe a sigh of relief. Or just breathe, period.

The Wrides will be back with Wride Palace, where you'll be able to skate, bowl, dance, and enjoy yourselves, you and your civilian and servicemen husbands, boyfriends, fathers . . . and I'm not forgetting there were some servicewomen, too. Come to Wride Palace, ladies, and have a drink on them!

Thanks for a wonderful war, listeners. I wish you peace, as my daughter Darie would say: I will never, ever forget you, ever!

Here she is, folks, for the last time.

> If our bombs stopped the killing,
>   clap your hands!
> If V-J Day was thrilling,
>   clap your hands,
> If you're glad we won the war,
>   glad they won't be back for more,
> Slap your sides,
> Thank you, Wrides,
> Clap your hands.

I never saw Daria again.